Matching You with Love

(All's Fair in Love and Sports)

Julie L. Spencer
and
Audi Lynn Anderson

CONTENTS

Chapter One—Taylor—Justifiable

"Seriously, bro, hook me up." Kade punched my shoulder as if that would make me change my mind.

"Dude, she's my best friend." I punched him back. "I wouldn't set you up with her if you were the last two humans on earth."

As I stepped down the front porch stairs of our modest home, I dreaded having to introduce my long-estranged twin brother to my next-door neighbor, the sweetest girl I'd ever met. This town had been my refuge from the life we'd known back in Nashville. Two years without drama, and now, in the spring of my senior year, he comes waltzing back into my life as if nothing ever happened.

"When are you gonna forgive me, Tay?" Kade asked, remorse and hurt creeping into his otherwise cocky demeanor. "Seriously, haven't I done my time?"

"Kade, I'm not sure I can ever forgive you." I kept walking away, knowing he'd follow whether I wanted him to or not.

"Taylor," he called to me when I'd only made it four feet down the driveway.

He meant business when he hauled out the big guns and called me by given name. Nobody called me Taylor. I'd been Tay since I could remember.

"Don't do this, man," he said. "We've been apart long enough, don't you think?"

"Kade, I finally have real friends who don't know you exist. I've never told any of these guys about you. I don't want you screwing up my life again."

"That's harsh." Kade scuffed his foot on the sidewalk.

Here in Clarksville nobody had ever judged me because I was Kade's brother.

I turned to confront him. "Can't we just stick to the plan—call you my cousin who came to live with us because your parents are going through a divorce?"

"Do you honestly think people are going to believe that?" Kade raised his eyebrows. "We may be fraternal, but we still look like twins."

"No, Kade, we don't. I would never wear my hair that long." I lifted one of his rock star wannabe shaggy curls, then glanced at his upper arm. "I don't dress in black clothes, and I can't imagine getting a tattoo."

"Don't dis the tat. This baby's a work of art." Kade lifted the sleeve of his faded Buxton Peak concert T-shirt to reveal a tattoo of their logo.

Obsessed much?

"How did you even get that?" I asked. "We're not eighteen yet."

"I got a fake ID, bro."

Of course he did. Why was I even surprised?

"See, and that is why I will never let you date my

best friend." I started checking off indiscretions on my fingers. "Dishonesty, theft, selling drugs, using drugs—"

He cut me off. "I have been clean for two years."

"Only because you've been locked up," I said, stepping closer and getting in his face. "Now that you're out, who's to say you aren't going right back into your old ways?"

"I'll prove it to you," Kade said. "I won't let you down this time."

"Prove it by pretending to be my cousin and don't screw up my life again."

"Now who's being dishonest?"

Dang, he had me.

"In this case, it's justifiable," I said.

"Yeah, well, mine was too." His gaze lowered again. "You don't know the whole story. And if you did, you'd be thanking me."

"I doubt that," I grumbled. I understood that he deserved a second chance, but not at the expense of my best friend. "I'll try to forgive you, but I'm not setting you up with Gracie."

"Whatever, *cuz*." Kade bumped his shoulder against mine. "Introduce me to your best friend, and I will try not to flirt with her."

"Thank you." I led him next door and knocked on the screen.

She bounded down the hall, squealing with

excitement. "He's here, he's here, he's here!"

"You told her I was coming?" Kade asked.

"I had to have an excuse why I missed her tennis match this morning."

"Do you attend all her tennis matches?"

"Yeah…" I said.

"And you claim you're just friends?"

"Best friends," I corrected him. "There's a difference."

"Right, we'll go with that."

Gracie swung open the door with enthusiasm, a grin spread across her face.

"Hello, gorgeous," Kade said.

Apparently, Kade had a nonexistent short-term memory because he forgot about the promise he'd just made not to flirt with her. She giggled in response.

"Gracie, this is my cousin, Kade." I cringed as the lie fell from my lips. "Kade, this is my best friend, Gracie."

Chapter Two—Gracie—Lucky

"Nice to meet you, Kade." I was beyond excited to meet Taylor's cousin. I knew very little about his family as close as we were. Taylor and I have been best friends for two years, but he didn't talk about anyone other than his immediate household and his Grandma Kendrick. Even on his trips to see his dad during school breaks, Tay never talked about him, and I figured it was better not to ask.

"Likewise," Kade said. "I've heard a lot about you."

Taylor elbowed him in the side, and Kade let out a nervous laugh.

"I'm sorry I didn't make it to your tennis match this morning," Taylor said, shuffling his feet on the porch's wood planking and shoving his hands into the pockets of his khaki shorts.

Taylor seemed nervous and more apologetic than he normally would when he missed one of my matches. I mean, I was sad he wasn't there, but I understood when something came up, especially something as exciting as seeing a cousin for the first time in years.

"That's okay," I said with a wave of my hand. "I'm happy you were able to go pick up your cousin. I can totally tell that you guys are cousins, by the way. You look exactly alike." I looked a lot like my cousin Veronica, but the resemblance between Taylor and Kade was on a whole new level.

"Told you," Kade said to Taylor. Kade's smoldering eyes, so similar to Taylor's, hid beneath disheveled brown curls that brushed just below his jawline.

"Nah," Taylor answered. "I would never wear my hair that long."

"And you don't dress in all black either." I looked Kade up and down. He wore dark, ripped jeans with an incredibly tight Buxton Peak shirt that emphasized his muscles in an all too tempting way. Kade certainly pulled off the bad-boy, rock-star vibe. Girls would no doubt flock to him at school on Monday.

"See, she knows me." Taylor raised his eyebrows at his cousin as if saying I told you so.

My classy best friend, Taylor, was more preppy with his collared shirt and khaki shorts. His clean-cut hair had a side part and the thick locks shone in the sunshine. He belonged at a country club on the golf course, with high-end clubs and his own caddy.

"Well, I can't wait for her to get to know *me*." Although Kade spoke to his cousin, his message was clearly directed my way. A smile spread across Kade's face as he brushed his thick brown curls out of his eyes and gave me a wink. As he moved, his cologne washed over me.

"Tay, you didn't tell me how hot your cousin is," I said to Taylor while flirtatiously glancing at Kade out of the corner of my eyes. Maybe it was a bit bold, and definitely not my normal go to, but there was something about this Kade and Taylor combo that was throwing me off balance.

"Well, gee, if he's hot and we look just alike, does that mean you think that I'm hot, too?"

"Oh please, you're my best friend. I could never think that you were hot." I jostled Tay's shoulder playfully, knowing it was a lie since I'd had a crush on him since we first met.

The disappointment on Taylor's face was evident that he was offended by my statement. I needed to soften the blow while also not giving away my secret infatuation with him. "But now that I know how hot your cousin is, I might have to take a closer look at you."

I used my hands to make a finger frame, focusing on his face as I pretended to zoom in and out. We both chuckled, and the tension in the air was gone almost as quickly as it arrived. Crisis averted.

"Despite his good looks, it's not like you two would go out anyways," Kade said. "Otherwise it would have happened already."

"Yeah right, like you and I could ever go out. Not." Something about him saying that made me wish we could go out. I tried not to think of him that way. It would hurt too much if he didn't like me back.

"Well, a noncommittal make-out session would have been a good option too," Kade said.

"Come on, dude, not cool," Taylor groaned, smacking him in the arm again. "We're friends. I've told you this a million times already."

Kade had a point. Making out would have been a fun

option. Clearly, Taylor didn't want that though, and I wasn't about to lose him as a friend even though I wanted more.

"Yeah, we're just friends. Speaking of which, Tay, I'm totally going to have to set you up with one of my friends so that the four of us can go on a double date." Someone should be able to enjoy how amazing I already know Tay is. Besides, that would give me an excuse to go out with Taylor without really going out with him. I loved double dates for this very reason.

"Does that mean you want to go on a date with me?" Kade asked.

"Gee, I should probably wait for you to ask me that huh?" I bit my lower lip, pretending to be coy. I flipped my hair over my shoulder and placed my fist on my popped out hip, trying my best to show confidence.

"You're a blunt one, aren't you?" Kade asked.

"You don't know the half of it," Taylor said under his breath. He put his hands behind his head and didn't try to hide his obvious annoyance with his cousin.

"Gracie, would you like to go on a date with me?"

"Yes!" I blurted out. Realizing I should take it back a notch, I cleared my throat and said calmly, "That would be lovely, thank you."

Taylor rolled his eyes and grumbled something under his breath again, but I couldn't hear what he said. I would have to ask him about what his deal was later.

"What's your favorite restaurant?" Kade asked, either completely unaware of Taylor's distaste for the situation or openly choosing to ignore it.

"That's not a very fun first date, now is it? Maybe something like mini golf or hiking instead."

"Wow, she is an absolute athlete like you, Tay," Kade said.

Taylor chose to ignore his comment. "Maybe you should figure out which one of your friends you're going to set me up with before you decide where we're going on our double date."

"True. Okay, I'll have to think about that. What color hair should the girl have? Should she be an athlete? Or should she be an artsy type?"

"I guess, hair like yours." He brushed a piece of my hair behind my ear. I held my breath as his fingertips felt like electricity on my cheek.

A slow smile crept across Taylor's face as if he was deep in thought. He quickly pulled his hand back and cleared his throat, "And for the rest of it, surprise me. If she's anything like you, I'm sure we'll get along just fine."

There was awkward silence for a few seconds before Kade said, "It was nice to meet you, gorgeous—I mean Gracie—but we should probably get going to help *Aunt* Rhonda with dinner. I look forward to our date once we find a hottie for Tay." Kade swung his arm around Taylor's shoulders, and Taylor grimaced before forcing a smile and stepping aside so Kade was no longer touching him.

Taylor glanced over at me and said, "Let me know if

you find a friend willing to go out with me."

"Very funny, you know any girl is more than willing," I responded and blew him a kiss as they walked away, back across the lawn to Taylor's house.

As soon as they went inside, I whipped out my phone to text my best girlfriend Maddie. *You are never going to believe this! How is this even happening right now? Tay's cousin came to live with him, and he is totally hottt!!! And get this, he asked me out! I already thought I was lucky having the hottest guy in school for my neighbor and best friend, but now I also get to be around his equally hot cousin? Thank you, universe, for blessing me this fine afternoon!*

My fingers hovered over the keys, wanting to text my other best girlfriend, Laura, but reminded myself for the billionth time that she still wasn't speaking to me.

I decided to look through my contacts to find a date for Tay. I was running out of options at school since I'd set him up so many times, but I just made a new friend, Hannah, at one of the shops downtown and decided to text her.

I slid the phone back into my pocket and hurried to my room, jumping onto my bed to stare at the Buxton Peak poster on my ceiling. I usually did my best thinking when I was looking at that poster because it reminded me of Taylor. His taking me to their concert in Nashville for my seventeenth birthday had been the highlight of my summer last year.

I had hoped that I'd have the guts to tell him how I really felt, but if he didn't like me back, I would have had a sour memory tied with one of my best. Not to mention the hour-long car ride back that would have been incredibly awkward otherwise.

My phone buzzed. It was Hannah saying she would love to go on a double date if it meant Taylor Kendrick would be her date. As I suspected, mini golf sounded fun to her.

"Wish he was mine." I put my phone down while I allowed myself to get lost again in my memories with Taylor before heading over to his house to let the guys know the plan.

Chapter Three—Taylor—Paul Reed Smith

"What the heck was that all about?" I smacked Kade on the arm. We'd barely stepped off the porch at Gracie's, and I was ready to have a throw-down fight with my twin. "You promised you weren't going to flirt with Gracie."

"I said I would *try* not to flirt with her." Kade smacked me back. "There's a difference."

"Whatever. I knew it was a bad idea having you come live here." We'd crossed the yards between Gracie's house and ours, and I opened the screen door, letting it fall closed behind me.

"Where would you want me to live?" Kade asked, not calling me out for the door hitting his shoulder.

"I don't know," I said. "With Dad, maybe?"

"That's where I got in trouble in the first place. Do you want me around my old friends?"

"You choose who to hang out with." I bypassed the kitchen, knowing Mom was bringing home food in an hour. I didn't want to disturb her spotless masterpiece she paid a cleaning lady to maintain as if she weren't raising five children.

"Well, I *choose* to hang out with you. My brother." Kade followed me, relentlessly worming his way back into my otherwise perfect new life.

16

"Don't call me that." I turned on him. "You're my cousin, remember?"

"Right, because I'm just supposed to forget about the first fifteen years of my life when I was your twin and the past two years while I was in juvie and you barely came to visit me. I was less than an hour away."

"I've moved on with my life." I made my point by continuing down the hall to the staircase.

"Yeah, well, you're going to have to fit me back in to your new life." He continued following me.

"You can start by wearing nicer clothes and cutting your hair," I suggested.

"Then people really will think we're twins."

He had a point.

"Fine, keep your ripped jeans and leave your hair long like a rock star." I took the stairs two at a time, but he was relentless in his pursuit.

"I love rock stars. Speaking of which, can I play your PRS? I miss that little baby." Kade bypassed his own bedroom, which already had his personal items organized exactly how Mom thought he would want them.

He had a lot of nerve asking to play my guitar after what he did. "Do you even remember how to play?" I entered my own bedroom, resigned that I would get zero privacy for the next few months of my life before heading to Stanford for college. My twin was attempting to make up for lost time together.

"Just like riding a bike." Kade strode over to the guitar stand in the corner of my room and picked up the one-of-a-kind Paul Reed Smith electric guitar, signed by Ian Taylor himself, the man I was named after.

My mom always said my dad loved Ian and his rock band more than he loved her. Guess that's why they lived in separate homes now. Mom got tired of always being second choice. They could use Grandma Kendrick, and her heart attack as the excuse. But none of the kids believed that. At least our mom and dad were still married, and still crazy about each other, even if they no longer lived together.

I lay down on my bed and grabbed a tennis ball. I threw it toward the ceiling and watched it fall neatly back into my hand, over and over.

Kade plugged in the amp and let the reverb fill my spacious bedroom. My eyes closed involuntarily. I might not have my brother's talent, but I could appreciate listening to him play. Took me back to a simpler time in my life.

Within a few minutes, our sixteen-year-old brother, Clay, entered my room and sat on the floor at Kade's feet, gazing up at him with hero worship in his eyes. Our older brother, Sean, home from college in celebration of Kade getting out of juvie came in and plopped into the giant beanbag in the corner. Lastly, little Reina skipped into the room, climbed onto my bed and snuggled into my arms. Her hand reached close to her face, the thumb twitching to her mouth.

I grunted at her, reminding her subtly to remember her age. "Kindergarteners don't suck their thumbs."

"I know that." Reina pulled her hand away from her face and tucked it behind her back.

For a few moments, we all listened while our brother played guitar—

Until suddenly, another face appeared in the doorway to my bedroom. I sat up in surprise. "Gracie, what are you doing here?"

Chapter Four—Gracie—Poster Child

Taylor's face lit up with a smile, and his little sister clamored to extricate herself from his arms when she saw me.

"Gracie!" Little Reina scrambled off the bed and ran across the spacious room, jumping into my arms. I laughed as she wrapped her arms around my neck.

"Didn't know I was missing a concert," I said, leaning against the doorway of Taylor's bedroom. I shifted the heavy six-year-old onto my hip.

The music stopped and Kade placed his hand across the strings of the guitar he was holding, silencing the reverb.

I'd let myself into Taylor's back door and through the kitchen as I always did, and heard loud music from upstairs. I was surprised to see that they were all gathered around Kade.

"Did you know Kade is here?" Reina asked, as if Kade wasn't right in front of me. "I haven't seen him in years!"

"It's only been a few months since you saw me, Ray." Kade switched off the amp to stop the sound altogether.

"Don't let me stop you from playing," I said. "Nice to see that guitar getting some use. Tay never plays it."

I carried Reina across the room and sat on Taylor's bed. Their younger brother, Clay, sat on the floor at Kade's feet as if he idolized his cousin.

"Hey, that thing's a collector's item," Taylor defended. "It's going to be worth something someday."

"It's worth something now, idiot." Their older brother, Sean, said from the beanbag in the corner. "It's a custom, private stock Paul Reed Smith guitar that is signed by Ian Taylor. There is nothing else like it in the world."

I glanced up at the poster above Taylor's bed, and his eyes followed mine. "How did you manage to get that guitar, anyway?"

"When Ian found out I was named after him, he gave it to me as a birthday present," Taylor said, still gazing at the poster where the rock band, Buxton Peak, stood in a pose worthy of a world-renowned boy band with a hint of rock god thrown in. They were a little younger in the photo than they were now, but it was a great poster. It was even matted and framed.

For the first time, I realized the poster wasn't just signed by the band members. It had personalized autographs written *to* Taylor. Dang. I set Reina on the bed and rose to get a closer look.

Happy birthday, little Tay. Love, Andy Smith. That was signed next to the band's bassist. *Tay, thanks for screaming at our concert. Gonna git you some headphones! Love, Nathanial Jackson.* That was next to their drummer. *Love you, Tay. Happy first birthday.* That was scrawled next to the band's lead guitarist, Kai

Burton. And last was a larger signature next to their front man, Ian Taylor, who must have been the guy who gifted the poster along with the guitar. *So cool that your parents named you after me, Little Tay. Love you, buddy. —Ian Taylor*

"A guitar is a pretty expensive first birthday gift," I said, turning back to Taylor.

"Ian's a billionaire," Taylor dismissed my concern. "He can afford it."

"Wanna hear me play it?" Kade asked me but looked to Taylor, almost as if getting his permission. They glared at each other for a moment, and I sensed more tension between the two of them.

"Whatever," Taylor mumbled and looked away. He lay on his bed and tossed a tennis ball into the air, letting it fall back into his hand. I wanted to comfort him but decided he and I could talk later when we could be alone. My best friend was having a tough day, and I needed to find out why.

As he continued tossing the ball in the air, I turned back to Kade. "I'd love to hear you play."

No one else seemed to notice the tension between Taylor and their cousin. We all settled into our spots, and Kade turned the amplifier back on.

Without thinking about it, I leaned against Taylor's headboard and pulled my feet up on the bed.

Taylor stilled for a second in response to me practically cuddled up by his side. He leaned his shoulder against my leg and glanced up at me, vulnerability in his eyes. I wondered if the tension between him and his cousin had anything to do with Kade flirting with me. Such a protective best friend.

I winked at Taylor, then faced Kade as the sound of reverb filled the room. Taylor resumed throwing his ball.

Kade was seriously talented on the guitar. No wonder the family was gathered around to listen. I was caught up in the music as he played songs from Aerosmith, Bon Jovi, Chuck Berry, Eddie Van Halen, Guns N' Roses, Carlos Santana, and Buxton Peak. He played Kai Burton's solo from their most popular song, *Passing through Eternity*, so well that I'd swear I was listening to a recording.

That was Taylor's favorite song, so he listened to it a lot. I guess if I were named after a rock star, his band would become my favorite band also.

After a little while of listening, a door slammed downstairs, and Rhonda called up to us. "Kids, I brought pizza."

"Pizza!" Clay hopped off the floor and headed out of the room. Sixteen-year-old boys were perpetually hungry.

"Pizza, pizza, pizza!" Reina slid down from the bed and followed her brother.

"Dang, you'd think they'd never been fed before." As Kade turned off the amp and put the guitar in its stand, I caught Taylor's tennis ball mid-throw.

"Wanna go hit some balls after dinner?" I asked

Taylor quietly, speaking to just him.

"I would *love* that." Taylor glanced up at me, his brown eyes smoldering. Dang, I wish he liked me as more than a friend.

When Kade cleared his throat from across the room, Taylor sat up and glared at him. "Don't even think about it. You can have your date with Gracie another day. Tennis is *our* thing."

"Yeah, tennis is *our* thing," I teased as Taylor swung his legs over the side of the bed. I stood to get out of his way and helped him to his feet.

"Hey, have you figured out who you're going to set me up with yet?" Taylor asked.

"Yes!" I realized I hadn't told him the reason I came over. "My friend Hannah from one of the shops downtown. She said she's free on Friday night if you're both up for some mini golf?"

"Whoever isn't up for mini golf?" Kade asked with sarcastic enthusiasm. I wondered if his idea of fun on a Friday night involved something stronger than mini golf.

"Yes, Friday sounds perfect." Taylor put his hand on the small of my back, leading me out into the hallway. "Let's eat some pizza and then head over to the courts, okay?"

Taylor was looking at me intensely, as if he was trying to communicate something he didn't want to say in front of his cousin. This wasn't like Taylor, and I hoped he would be willing to open up when we got to the courts.

"Whenever you're ready, Tay," I responded, looking him straight in the eyes for several seconds, hoping to convey the message that I was ready to listen as soon as he was ready to talk.

Kade coughed from the doorway to Taylor's bedroom. "So, gorgeous—I mean Gracie—I hear we have *chemistry* together." Kade's emphasis on chemistry was purposely provocative.

Through nearly clenched teeth, Taylor said to me, "I went ahead and shared our schedules with Kade."

"That was very thoughtful of you, Tay." I patted Taylor on the shoulder. "I'll make sure Kade has a great first day at his new school."

"I bet you will." Kade's suggestive comment earned him a punch in the arm from his cousin.

As I skipped down the stairs ahead of them, I could hear Kade and Taylor talking aggressively to each other under their breaths. Maybe they *weren't* rekindling their childhood friendship.

When I walked into the kitchen, Rhonda offered me a slice of pizza, which I gladly accepted. She looked tired, and I marveled at how brave she was to take on one more mouth to feed when she was already raising four kids as a single mom.

There was a possibility that my mom might soon know how that felt, and I wasn't ready. My parents hadn't officially split up yet, but the threat hung over our family like an ominous cloud. At least my best friend would be able to comfort me through my parents' divorce, if it came down to that.

I didn't want it to come down to that.

Chapter Five—Taylor—Wicked Serve

"Geesh, Tay, aren't you even going to wait until I have a chance to unpack a racket?" Gracie asked as she set down her bag and unzipped the compartment with her favorite rackets. She kept them lined up in order of string tension and practiced with a different racket each day to gradually break them all in. By the time she got to a tournament, most of the rackets in her bag were optimized.

"No," I grumbled. "Stay over here. I don't want to hit you."

"Okaaay…" She slipped behind me and to the side, keeping a wide berth.

I tossed the next ball into the air and smacked it as hard as I could, not caring whether the serve was accurate. This wasn't practice for me; it was blowing off steam, shaking off the aggression in my heart. Every ball I hit, I imagined Kade's smirk, and I just wanted to smack him. Punch him. Hit him. Each ball had his face.

Then I realized his face was my face. Hating him was hurting us both. I screamed and almost smashed my racket against the court. Thankfully, I kept my temper at bay.

"Hey." Gracie's soft voice was closer than I was expecting. She was brave to come this close to a guy who was a hair away from completely losing his temper. That woke me up. "You want to talk about it?"

27

"Not really." I lowered my racket and let my arms go slack at my sides.

"I take it Kade moving in with you guys wasn't your idea?" Her compassion was undeserved, especially when I responded with sarcasm.

"Gee, what makes you think that?"

She didn't answer, just pursed her lips and lifted her chin. Her long, blonde hair pulled into a ponytail fell down her back.

"Sorry, I didn't mean to be a prick."

"Do you remember the first day we came here to the tennis courts two years ago?" she asked.

"Of course." I knew where she was going with this. "I watched you from my bedroom window as you stormed out of your house, carrying your tennis bag and wiping tears from your face."

"And do you remember why I was crying and storming from my house?"

"Because your parents were fighting again."

"And what did you do?" she asked.

"I followed you here like a stalker." I chuckled, and she joined in, breaking the tension.

"You listened," she said. "Even though we barely knew each other, and I was a blubbering mess, we sat here on the court and you listened as I told you about my horrible day."

"And you smiled afterward."

"And then we played tennis together for an hour," she said.

"And I was terrible."

"You had room for improvement." She raised her eyebrows. I knew she wasn't just talking about tennis anymore.

"He's a jerk, okay? I don't want him living with me because he's gonna ruin my life again when I finally have normal friends and a normal house and a normal life, and I don't want his drama."

"See, don't you feel better now, getting that off your chest? If I know anything about my best friend, it's that you won't let some jerk ruin your life."

"Easier said than done when the jerk is family," I grumbled.

"I'm never going to choose him over you, if that's what you're worried about. One date with your cousin isn't going to change the friendship you and I share."

"Unless you fall in love, grow up and get married." I was trying to make a joke, but the thought of them together that way was revolting. She deserved a guy better than him.

"Well, if that were the case, I'd have the best cousin-in-law ever."

I almost corrected her that she'd have the best brother-in-law ever, but I kept myself in check. I held up my racket. "You ready to beat the crap out of me?"

"Definitely." Before heading over to the other side

of the court, Gracie tucked herself into my arms, and we held each other for a long moment.

I wished she could be in my arms every day and go on dates with me, not my twin brother. But she didn't like me that way, and I could understand why. I was boring and normal. Kade was a sexy, brooding bad boy with the potential to be a rock star someday. If he hadn't gotten into trouble when he did, he'd probably already be a rock star. With our dad and his connections, Kade could pick his venue.

No girl would choose me over him, not even my best friend. I pulled back and handed her the ball I'd had in my hand. "You can serve first."

Chapter Six—Gracie—Chemistry

"Hey, gorgeous—I mean Gracie," said the voice behind my locker door. I moved it slightly to see Kade leaning his shoulder against the lockers next to mine. His hair was styled in the same disheveled curls, but today he was sporting a seriously expensive looking leather jacket over his dark clothing.

"Hey, yourself," I replied as I pulled my chemistry book out of my locker. "You know, you look like a genuine rock star."

"Do I now?" Kade chuckled. "Well, I'm sure there is a reason for that. Maybe, just maybe, I'm an even bigger Buxton Peak fan than my dear *cousin*." Was he making fun of Taylor? I wanted to call him out, but I decided to stay on Kade's good side so I could possibly help fix what was broken between them.

"I don't know about that," I said, only half teasing. "Tay knows all of their songs and goes to a lot of their concerts. Even backstage at some."

"Does he really?" Kade's eyes widened, and he mumbled, "Surprised he went without me." Kade almost seemed offended or hurt.

"Okay, no need to be jealous. Kind of hard to attend concerts together when you live far away. He's only taken me once, if that makes you feel any better."

"It does make me feel better." Kade seemed to pull

himself together. "You are after all his *best* friend."

"That's right." I turned back to my locker to grab my lab notebook so we could head to chemistry class. "I'm his best friend." Was I trying to convince myself? Or Kade?

"How about we shut this scrapbook—I mean locker—and head to class, hmm?" Kade nodded toward my open locker with all the magnets, paper crafts, and pictures with friends, most of which included Taylor. Huh, I'd never noticed there were so many pictures of me and Taylor in my locker. I wondered if Taylor ever noticed.

"Scrapbook?" My jaw dropped with feigned offense.

"Yeah, it looks like a scrapbooking company held their annual meeting inside your locker."

"Just so you know"—I closed my locker and offered a flirtatious grin—"I love my *scrapbook* inspired locker."

"I'm sure you do." Kade raised his eyebrows knowingly. I wondered if he was referencing all the pictures with Taylor, but I didn't ask. He seemed to see right through me. I wondered if I should worry about losing my heart to him or worry that he would call me out for my attraction to Taylor.

I turned away from my locker, and we walked down the hall together, drawing attention from our classmates. It was a small enough school that everyone knew Kade was Taylor's cousin. They all knew that Taylor and I were best friends, so logically I would also be friends with his cousin. Right? "Everyone is staring at us," I said under my breath.

Kade smirked. "Maybe they just wish they were me so they could have *chemistry* with you too."

"Very funny." My cheeks flushed, and I lowered my gaze. More likely they all wished they were *me* so they could get close to the mysterious hot guy who was my new next-door neighbor.

"You know I was just joking," Kade said solemnly. "I'm sure you're a fantastic person. I mean Tay seems to really like you, and he normally has better luck with friends than I do."

"You seem to know more about me than I know about you." I glanced over at Kade, and his brows were furrowed as if deep in thought. What didn't make sense was that Taylor had never mentioned Kade before. Taylor was like that about a lot of his family members, but Kade seemed to be an especially touchy subject for him. "You coming here must have been a sudden thing for him. I noticed you two don't have *chemistry* together."

Kade was silent the entire rest of the way to our classroom. When I reached for the handle, Kade put his arm up, preventing me from opening the door. He looked directly into my eyes and said in a low voice, "Not everything Tay says about me is true. I know you're best friends, but he has some big misunderstandings about me. I don't want you to see me differently because he's still angry at me for something I did years ago."

I grabbed Kade's free hand and held it between

mine. I stepped closer so I was less than a foot away from him. I wanted him to be the only one who could hear me. "I trust Tay with nearly everything, but he also knows I think for myself. I'm not going to pre-judge you, Kade. That's not who I am. My friendship with Tay is completely separate from my friendship with you. Tay respects my friendships, even if he doesn't always understand them. I'm sure you'll be no exception." I let go of his hand and took one step backward.

Before Kade opened the door to the chemistry classroom, he said, "You're different from what I expected."

"Yeah, well you're different from what I expected because I didn't even know you existed." I offered him a quick wink. "Shall we see about our *chemistry* class then?"

Just as I was entering the classroom, I looked over his shoulder and noticed Laura, my former best friend. She had her camera out, which was normal for the photographer of the school newspaper, but she had her eyes and camera pointed directly at me. What was her deal? Was she taking pictures of people in the hallway? Maybe she was taking pictures of Kade since he was the new guy.

The school paper had taken over Laura's life, and she no longer had room for me. Or maybe I no longer had room for her.

We stopped hanging out after she quit the tennis team our sophomore year. Thankfully, that was about the time Taylor and I became friends, so he was able to fill that void.

Her leaving had been a loss for our team because her natural talent and skills rivaled my own. She could have easily been an all-state champion. But her leaving meant I lost one of my best friends too. I still didn't know what I did to make her so mad at me. We used to be inseparable.

I was way overthinking this. I offered her a half smile and ducked into my classroom.

Chapter Seven—Taylor
Give Him a Chance

"How was your first day of school, guys?" Mom asked when we walked in the door.

"Wasn't my first day of school," I mumbled, dropping my backpack in the mudroom and heading straight for the refrigerator.

"That was probably the best day of school ever in my life," Kade said. He leaned against the kitchen island and reached for a banana from the fruit basket. "You'd be surprised how much you miss something as mundane as school when you're kept away for two years."

"Your own fault." I couldn't help being rude even though I knew to rein myself in.

"Tay, enough of that." Mom gave me that look.

"Sorry, Mom," I said under my breath, not nearly as sorry as I should have been.

"Apologize to your brother, not me."

"What, are we in preschool?" I asked.

"You tell me. You're the one acting like a four-year-old."

I ignored my mom and glared across the room at my twin brother, daring him to demand an apology. He took the initiative to change the subject, essentially letting me off the hook.

"Clarksville High School has a great band program," Kade said, releasing my gaze and looking over at our mom. "I wish I'd been here during basketball season because they apparently have a jazz band that rocks. Right now, the seniors aren't doing much except hanging out while the kids practice songs for graduation and crap like that. A couple of the guys and I went into one of the practice rooms and jammed, plus, this chick named Maddie, who has a crazy awesome voice. She has a great twist on Uncle Ian's songs. Totally took me back, ya know?"

"I know Maddie. She's a really sweet girl," Mom said. "But are the rest of them good kids?" Mom didn't even try to hide her suspicion. I was sure she was just as leery of Kade getting involved in the wrong crowd as I was.

"Doesn't matter." Kade's tone was defensive. "I'm not gonna do nothin'. Geesh, Mom. Besides, I just met 'em today. How would I know?"

"I just want you to be careful." She picked up her oven mitts and opened the door, allowing the heavenly aroma of lasagna to waft into the kitchen. She pulled off the foil to check if the lasagna was ready, turned the pan around for even heating, and pushed the casserole dish back in the oven.

"Yeah, make new friends, Kade." Kade's statement dripped with sarcasm. "But only the right kind of friends, is that it?"

"You don't need to be all defensive," Mom said,

37

closing the oven door. She placed the mitts on the counter and turned to my brother. "We just got you back, and I don't want to lose you again."

"I'm not goin' nowhere, okay?" Kade pushed past me and reached into the refrigerator for a Perrier, his strange go-to drink. I always suspected he used sparkling mineral water to hide a shot of vodka, but there was no alcohol in our house, that I knew of anyway. "I got homework. I'll be in my room."

Kade stopped in the mudroom to grab his backpack and headed for the stairs.

Mom sighed, and I felt bad for snapping at her.

"You need to let up on him, Tay," she said. "You're going to push him away, and he may never come back."

"What if I didn't want him to come back?" I couldn't meet her gaze.

"You don't mean that." Her soft voice offered compassion. "He's your twin brother. If you weren't meant to be together, you wouldn't have been born at the same time."

I'd heard that argument all my life. "Mom, we have nothing in common."

"That's not the real issue, though, is it?" Mom saw right through me.

My answer was barely a whisper, and I was afraid I'd start crying if I wasn't careful. "I don't know if I can forgive him," I admitted. "He's the reason we only get to see Dad every few months instead of every day."

"You know your dad and I needed space from each other," Mom said. "Our separation isn't just about Kade. It may feel that way, but this has been better for us."

"What about what's better for us kids?" I asked.

Mom gulped. "You can go see your dad whenever he's not on tour. You can take time off school if you want so you can go see him."

"Yeah, I know…"

"Right now, he's working. You wouldn't see him every day anyway. At least being here, we can avoid all the craziness of Nashville."

"True."

"Let Kade prove to you that he's changed, Tay." Mom came around the kitchen island and took me in her arms. I reluctantly let her hold me, inhaling the subtle French perfume she always wore.

"I'll try, okay?" I settled into a comfortable hug with my mom, allowing a rare show of affection. "Maybe I can go see if he needs help with homework or something."

"That's a great idea." She gave me one more hug, then released me from her arms.

I grabbed my backpack and headed up to Kade's room. Without knocking, I opened his door and found him lying on his bed, a copy of *The Great Gatsby* in his hand.

"Need the SparkNotes version?" I asked, knowing

39

that book was dreadfully dull to most seventeen-year-old boys but, more importantly, knowing that our midterm test was next week. He would need to cram several weeks' worth of reading into only a few days.

"I really like it so far." Kade turned the book around and glanced at the cover. "I've grown to appreciate good books."

"Who are you, and what did you do with my twin brother?" I dropped my backpack on the floor and pulled out my own copy of *The Great Gatsby*. I had about ten pages left and was behind. Might as well join him. I climbed over Kade and lay down on the other side of his queen bed.

"Your twin brother went to a juvenile detention center and came back as your cousin, remember?" His sarcasm barely hid the hurt that was probably clawing at his heart.

"If only we could turn back time." I settled onto his extra pillow, and we read in companionable silence until Mom called us down for dinner.

Chapter Eight—Gracie—Mini golf

"I hope you're all ready to get your butts kicked," I said as I practiced my putting swing.

"In your dreams, short stuff." Hannah was tall like Taylor and Kade. She had a dark complexion, with big, brown eyes and natural makeup. Her hair was pulled back in a ponytail, and she wore jeans and sneakers with a graphic T-shirt.

"Hey now, slow down," Kade said. "Save the trash talk for the course." Dressed in black jeans and T-shirt, Kade looked more like Hannah's date than mine.

Taylor chuckled but didn't say anything. I wondered if he felt uncomfortable being here with Kade. He certainly seemed out of place, standing beside the two of them. His khakis, button up, and cardigan sweater mirrored mine, and I tried to shake off the sense that we were matched incorrectly on this date.

We walked to the first hole with our color-specific balls so that we could tell them apart. The mini-golf course was lively, with several families and other couples on dates. The flashing lights from the animatronic pirates and birds combined with the adventurous water features made a fun, lighthearted atmosphere. Perfect for a first date, and for Kade and Taylor to hopefully relax around each other.

"So, who wants to go first?" Hannah asked.

"How about oldest to youngest?" I suggested. "Kade, when's your birthday?"

"June twenty-eighth," Kade said without hesitation, then glanced at Taylor, who looked like he was clenching his teeth.

"Huh, what are the odds that you and Taylor would have the same birthday?" I asked, also glancing at Taylor.

"Pretty slim, I would say, but stranger things have happened." Kade shrugged and cleared his throat.

"Guess our parents must have both had a party in October and gotten carried away," Taylor said with a sneer. Why did he always have to show such animosity toward Kade? I'd gotten to know him more through our chemistry class when he was assigned to be my lab partner. He'd been super helpful the whole week and was incredibly smart. I hadn't expected that with his rock-star bad-boy persona. He certainly didn't seem to be the jerk Taylor claimed he was.

"I wouldn't want to share a birthday," said Hannah. She seemed oblivious to the tension between our two dates. "I like to have a day dedicated to just me."

"Same," I agreed. "My birthday's July seventeenth. What about you, Hannah?"

"Mine's May thirteenth, so I'm the oldest. Why don't we go me, Taylor, Kade, then Gracie?" Hannah's question sounded more like a plan that was not up for discussion.

"Sounds great," Taylor said. "Let's do this." He held

out his hand, inviting Hannah to step up to the tee pad.

Hannah putted her ball close to the hole and offered Taylor a high five as he took her place. Why did that make me jealous? He wasn't my date.

Taylor's ball bounced off the brick barrier a few times but ended up on the green close to the hole.

Kade wasn't even close and had to re-hit his ball twice just to get it over the first hill.

"Alright, Gracie, let's put some of that trash talk to the test." Hannah sneered playfully.

I stepped up and set my hot pink ball down on the tee, lined up my shot, and, with one quick swing, got a hole in one.

"Boom!" I cheered, jumping to celebrate my awesome shot.

Kade lifted me in a hug of congratulations, and Hannah offered me a high five.

As we walked toward the end of the green to retrieve our balls, Taylor leaned close to me and asked, "It's that lucky charm I got you, isn't it?"

"I came prepared," I said with a wink, shaking my wrist so we could hear the charms jingle.

I looked down at the charm bracelet Taylor had given me on my sixteenth birthday, shortly after we became friends. Every now and then he would surprise me with a new charm. A tennis racket, of course, in remembrance of how we became friends, a music note to commemorate the day we went to a Buxton Peak concert together. Another charm was a stack of books for the late nights we spent together studying. There were others, but the most recent charm was declared to be my lucky charm. It was a circle with a mix of green and pink, our favorite colors, because we were so lucky to have found each other as best friends.

We kept playing through all eighteen holes, and predictably I won. Hannah was a close second, but Kade and Taylor hit their balls into the water so many times that we stopped counting their shots at hole ten.

"Well, now that I have been thoroughly reminded how bad I am at sports, how about some ice cream?" Kade suggested, wrapping his arm around my waist and leading me to the concession stand.

"Yes please," I said. "I always have a terrible sweet tooth, especially for peanut butter chocolate ice cream."

"I will gladly satiate that sweet tooth," Kade said in a sultry voice. I smacked his shoulder.

I looked back and noticed Taylor and Hannah were smiling at each other as they took our clubs and balls back to the main counter. They seemed to be hitting it off, sort of. I fought that same pang of jealousy even though I had been the one to set them up on this date in the first place. Hannah was a great person, but not good enough for my best friend.

Kade either didn't notice my frustration or chose to ignore my creased brows and distracted glare. He ordered our ice cream, and we sat at a nearby picnic table opposite each other as we waited for Hannah and Taylor to order theirs.

"Tell me the story about your necklace." Kade pointed to the heart I wore on a delicate chain. "You always seem to be wearing it."

"Tay got it for me this past Christmas." I fiddled with the heart between my fingers. "It says, *Omnia vincit amor*, which means *love conquers all*."

"Love, huh?" Kade smirked knowingly. I realized I needed to clarify the meaning.

"My parents fight a lot, and Tay got me this necklace to remind me that they love me, and deep down they probably still love each other. And at the end of the day, love is what gets us through our hard times."

Kade didn't say anything but stood and leaned over the table. With his face inches away from mine, I could smell his cologne. My heart pounded as I waited for his next move.

Gently, he brushed my fingers away from the words so he could read them, and a soft smile appeared on his face. He whispered the phrase as if he were saying it to himself. His glance shifted so that he was looking me in the eyes.

"Tay's really lucky to have you," Kade whispered. Then he kissed me on the forehead before settling back down on his side of the bench.

I was speechless. This was not the Kade that Taylor described to me, and the more I got to know Kade, the more I thought Taylor misunderstood him. I also realized that my relationship and interest with Kade had shifted since we'd met. Although I still found him extremely attractive, he was more like a brother to me.

Kade and I sat in silence across the picnic table from one another, eating our ice cream and waiting for Hannah and Taylor to bring their ice cream over and sit with us.

"Yum, give me a bite." Taylor leaned close when he sat beside me on the bench. "You always get peanut butter chocolate. My favorite."

As he took my cone, he handed me his, and I teased him. "If peanut butter chocolate is your favorite, why do you always get strawberry?" Without considering the notion that we were swapping spit, we traded back after I took a huge bite of his, scoring a large chunk of frozen strawberry.

Kade raised his eyebrows and smirked at me across the table, his eyes darting back and forth between me and Taylor. I wondered if he figured out I was secretly in love with his cousin?

Kade bumped his elbow gently against the girl who was supposedly on a date with Taylor and offered his cone to Hannah. "You wanna trade?"

Hannah wrinkled her nose. "No thanks, I don't like mint chocolate chip."

"That's okay, I don't like butter pecan either." Kade resumed eating his own ice cream.

The rest of the evening was lighthearted and playful, joking around and having fun. This no longer felt like a date other than when Taylor wrapped his arm around my back to snag the last bite of my cone.

As we were wiping off our table and getting ready to

leave, I noticed Laura near the edge of the patio, taking pictures of students from our high school as they obliviously played mini golf and ate ice cream.

She was often single-handedly in charge of running the entire school paper. She did everything from reporting, to photography, and right down to the editing.

I wondered what crazy project she had planned for this week's edition and how kids playing mini golf factored into her story. Guess I would have to wait for Monday during homeroom. The school paper was a major highlight every Monday morning, and that was in large credit to her diligence over the prior week.

After gathering up my used napkins, I threw them in the trash, then followed my friends to where Taylor had parked his car.

Kade opened the back door for me like a gentleman, and I slipped into the seat, wishing I could sit up front. Where I normally sat. When Taylor wasn't on a date with someone else.

Chapter Nine—Taylor—The Great Gatsby

"Dude, you didn't tell me I was missing a study session," Kade said, sliding into the seat beside me. Our dining room table was spread with textbooks and notebooks like it always was on Sunday afternoons. Just another part of my routine life that Kade was disrupting. He flopped his chemistry textbook on the table and spoke directly to Gracie. "Need any help?"

"Actually, I do," she said. I hadn't realized she was struggling. "I can't get these coefficients to balance. What am I doing wrong?" She slid her lab notebook across the table, and Kade placed hers beside his, glancing back and forth between the two. Was he really smart enough to know how to help her?

"Ah, you didn't account for the coefficients you used to balance the carbon atoms before you tried to balance the oxygen atoms." He slid both notebooks across the table to show where he'd already balanced the equation. "See, when you add coefficients to the product, you've now increased its number of oxygen atoms. If you add a coefficient of five to the oxygen molecule in the reactant, you'll have balanced the carbon and the oxygen, and the hydrogen should be obvious."

"Oh my gosh, that totally worked." Gracie sounded almost as surprised as I felt.

"Dang, how did you get so smart?" I asked my brother.

He shrugged. "I had a lot of time to study the past couple of years."

"Yeah, I guess you did," I mumbled, pulling out my dog-eared copy of *The Great Gatsby,* the dreadfully boring story of snobby rich people who swore too much and had more affairs than I could keep track of. They lived in Long Island mansions across the bay from each other on something called the East Egg and the West Egg. I was glad my family lived in a nice, normal house in a nice, normal neighborhood without all the drama of the uber rich. "Got any more chemistry questions? Or do you want to move on to the great American novel?"

"That was the only question stumping me," Gracie said. "We can move on." She also pulled out her copy of *The Great Gatsby*.

"Gracie and I are good with *chemistry*, aren't we?" Kade winked at Gracie. Jealousy flared inside me, and I almost shoved my brother off the chair beside me.

"Do you guys have *any* idea what you're going to write about in your Gatsby essays?" Gracie asked with exaggerated frustration. "I have far too many ideas."

Yeah right. She probably already had three different essay outlines started. She was one of the smartest girls I knew.

"Probably about how Fitzgerald clearly wanted to distinguish the transcendence of class over wealth in American society," Kade said.

Huh? This is definitely not the Kade I remembered. I wanted to ask him again how he got so smart, but in asking, I didn't want to make myself look stupid.

49

Kade continued. "It's a classic case of old money trumping new money despite the capitalist economy that rewards innovation."

"But I thought capitalism was bad." Gracie's brow creased.

"No, that's just what the people with *old* money want you to believe," Kade told her. "If it weren't for capitalism, you wouldn't be holding that iPhone in your hand, and Buxton Peak wouldn't be the greatest rock band on the planet."

Gracie threw her head back and laughed. "What does a rock band have to do with capitalism?"

"That rock band is a classic example of new money created on the premise of innovation and talent."

"What about the next generation after the rock band creates new money?" I asked, now fully engrossed in the discussion despite our complete derailment from the topic of *The Great Gatsby*. "Would the children of the rock stars be considered old money because they were living off the riches created by their parents?"

"Possibly…" Kade narrowed his eyes at me. "I suppose that depends on how the kids choose to invest their time and energy."

"And if they look down upon people who don't have money," Gracie pointed out.

"Or if they allow their wealth to justify their own corruption," I added, knowing Gracie wouldn't understand the reference but Kade would.

"Sometimes wealth enables people to fall into the

trap of drinking and doing drugs… and other bad things." Kade glanced at me, and I could tell we were no longer talking about a historic novel from the nineteen twenties.

"Like Gary Owens," Gracie said, pulling our focus away from each other. Kade and I both turned our attention to her, startled by the direction of her thoughts. "He was their drummer. Don't you remember?"

"He died before we were born," I said, confused. "We never met him."

"Obviously you never met him. Even with your backstage passes, there is only so much meeting that can happen. But you've heard of him, right?" Gracie's eyes darted back and forth between me and Kade.

"Yeah, of course." Kade snorted. I wondered if he'd mention the collector's memorabilia autographed by Gary that our dad had purchased at auction. "I mean, he was a great drummer."

"But going back to your original point," Gracie said. "If he hadn't gotten super rich, he might not have had access to drugs, and then he might be alive today."

"Yeah, it's good to be alive." Kade lowered his eyes and fiddled with the corner of his book. I wondered how close Kade had come to doing something over-the-top stupid. I could have lost him for real. Not just for two years. I needed to remember that.

"Unlike Gatsby, who was murdered," Gracie declared.

"Only because he took the fall for the person he loved the most," Kade mumbled, glancing at me again.

"What do you mean?" Gracie asked.

"Daisy was driving the car that killed Tom's mistress, but Gatsby took the blame," Kade said, lifting his gaze. "Sometimes people take the blame and pay the ultimate price."

"Like going to jail…" I choked out, again knowing Kade and I were talking about a completely different story than Gracie.

"Or in Gatsby's case, getting murdered." Gracie sighed. "Thanks, guys, you have really helped give me some direction for this essay. We're going to ace the exam, too."

As Gracie gathered up her books and notebooks, shoving them into her backpack, Kade and I sat in silence. I weighed the implication of his statement, realizing there was more to the story that had haunted me for two years.

What was Kade trying to tell me? *Took the fall for the person he loved the most?* What really happened the night Kade was arrested?

Chapter Ten—Gracie
The Newspaper Never Lies

"Did you figure out our chemistry homework this weekend?" Maddie asked, setting her stack of books on the desk beside mine. We were in homeroom first thing Monday morning. Some kids were frantically trying to finish incomplete assignments. She and I usually worked ahead so we didn't get overstressed from all of our other activities. Tennis for me, music for her. I'd won the entire tennis tournament for first singles on Saturday. Kade and Taylor both came to support me, which was super nice.

"Yeah, Kade joined Tay and me for our weekend study session, so he helped me figure it out." I thought back to our discussion at their dining room table. Kade joining us added an interesting dynamic to our normal routine. Taylor and I had gotten relaxed together these past two years, and Kade shook us out of our comfort zone.

"You and Kade have been spending a lot of time together." Maddie wiggled her eyebrows up and down.

"Well, he is my best friend's cousin, and they live in the same house, and we are neighbors, and we have class together, so odds are we would spend a lot of time together." Why was I being so defensive? Why did I suddenly want to put the idea of Kade and me to rest?

"I don't know, girl." Was she baiting me? She was

my best girlfriend, so she'd probably already figured out that I was secretly in love with Taylor but had never said anything.

"I will not deny that he is good looking," I said. "I mean have you seen him?"

Maddie chuckled. "Oh, I've seen him alright." The provocative desire came through in her voice.

"Yeah, I'm sure you have. You know, you've got natural talent just like him. Maybe you two should start an official rock band together?"

"That'd be something. He seems to enjoy jamming with the guys and me too. He is a whole new level of talent compared to the rest of the guys. What else do you know about him?"

"He's a super nice guy," I said. "Like, under the bad-boy, wanna-be rock star persona, he's almost as nice as Tay."

Maddie raised her eyebrows in disbelief. "Only *nice*?" She closed her chemistry textbook and placed her elbow on it so she could rest her head in her hand as she stared me down. "There is more to him than that. Spill."

"Okay, he is undoubtedly more flirtatious and forward than Tay, but they are both very smart and equally gorgeous."

"You mean sexy." Maddie smirked and winked.

I let out a sigh and stared at the ceiling. "Yes, I mean sexy."

Maybe I should match up Maddie with Kade. Knowing Maddie the way I did, I was sure she could figure out how to snag Kade without my expert matchmaking skills.

Maddie was absolutely stunning with her dark skin and natural hair. She almost always wore subtle makeup, white gold hoop earrings, and sustainable clothing from her minimalist capsule wardrobe. They would undoubtedly look great together.

She was the embodiment of authenticity. But she was also the embodiment of persistence, which meant she was never going to drop this topic without serious convincing.

The classroom door opened and a freshman on the school newspaper committee brought in a large stack of newspapers. I should have known there was trouble when I saw how nervous the freshman looked. He handed them to our homeroom teacher, Mr. Johnson, and hurried from the room.

Mr. Johnson let out a long sigh and glanced up at me with deep, sympathetic eyes. What was going on?

"Alright class, come and grab a paper off the desk if you want one, but please keep the noise down so others can continue working on their homework." After 30 years in the profession, Mr. Johnson had perfected his matter-of-fact tone.

I didn't even get halfway to Mr. Johnson's desk before my ex-boyfriend Jimmy blurted out, "So much for being in love with Sir Tay Kendrick, Miss Perfect."

I stopped in my tracks. In love? Miss Perfect? Was

he still upset that I dumped him two years ago? One of my classmates, Marie, turned to me with a smirk.

"Didn't take you long to latch on to the next hottie, now did it?" Marie asked.

"What are you guys talking about?" A nervous panic came over me.

"Umm, this." Maddie handed me her copy of the paper, a bit of hurt in her voice.

Front page of the paper, above the fold. *Our Newest Couple: Prom King and Queen?* Below were pictures of me and Kade. So many pictures. I unfolded the paper to see pictures of him leaning on the lockers beside mine as we gazed at each other. Photos of me holding his hand, mere inches from his face as I spoke to him. Photos of him at my tennis tournament cheering me on. The worst photo of all was the one of him kissing my forehead during our intimate conversation on our date Friday night.

I began reading the blatant lies about how Kade and I fell in love at first sight, that we have spent nearly every moment together from the time he arrived, and that our love was the kind that couples dreamed about.

There was even a supposed quote from me saying, "I knew Kade was the one for me the moment I saw him. He is so much like my best friend Taylor, but there was something about Kade that made me fall in love with him."

Another obviously falsified quote from Kade, read, "Gracie is the most amazing girl, and I have to thank my cousin Taylor for introducing me to the love of my life."

"This isn't true!" I panicked. How could they not see the misquotes from just the way neither of us would ever call Tay by his full name?

"I don't know, Gracie, I do see you guys together a lot." Heidi, from my tennis team, raised her eyebrows. "He was at our tennis tournament this weekend."

"Yeah, because Tay was there like he is at every tournament because he's my best friend." My voice cracked.

"He does look a lot like Tay though, dude," Jimmy said. "I mean you and Tay obviously friend-zoned each other a long time ago, or you'd be dating by now. He was the reason you and I broke up."

"I broke up with you because you're a selfish jerk who never supported me in anything and because you tried to get me into the back seat of your car." My anger toward Jimmy compounded my embarrassment and frustration. "This paper is lying. I am not dating Kade, nor am I even interested in dating Kade. And Tay and I did not friend-zone each other."

"You did just tell me you thought Kade was hot," Maddie reminded me.

"Just like every other girl in this school would say." How could Maddie not be backing me up? She was one of my best friends.

"Alright, kids, settle down," Mr. Johnson called out in an attempt to regain control of the class. "I'm sure there's a misunderstanding, and you all need to get back to your desks."

Nobody paid Mr. Johnson any attention, and the assault on my character and love life continued.

"How poetic that Miss Goody Two-shoes fell in love with a bad boy," Marie said.

"And Kade is obviously interested in you." Heidi held up the paper to show me the front page as if I hadn't already seen it. "I mean these pictures don't lie."

"They *do* lie." My voice cracked as I tried to hold back tears and keep my chin up.

"You just don't want to admit you're dating Kade," Jimmy continued his jabs. "How long did you think you could keep this a secret? Does Tay know about your little love affair, or will this be a surprise to him too? Maybe we should text him to see how he's taking this news."

"Shut up, Jimmy," I said through clenched teeth, tears welling in my eyes.

"Ah, come on, Gracie." Jimmy pointed at each picture. "Kade is literally kissing you in this picture, and you are the one holding his hand in this one. You walk to class together, hang out together every day, and obviously go on dates with each other. He even showed up to one of your dreadfully boring tennis matches."

"We are friends, nothing else," I snapped back.

"I've heard that one before," Jimmy said so intensely that I could feel his resentful scorn. "You want everyone to think you're so perfect, but underneath this façade you are broken. Maybe that's why Tay never made a move on you, even after you broke up with me for him. You're too difficult to be with anyway, so hats off and good luck to Kade. He has no idea what he's gotten himself into with you."

"Please stop," I begged almost inaudibly.

"It's so obvious you're in love with Kade." Jimmy kept taunting me, pushing me to admit the truth he already knew. "Why do you keep denying it?"

"Because I'm in love with Tay!" I blurted and instantly covered my mouth with both of my hands as I realized I could never take it back.

Everyone in the room fell silent, all eyes fixed on me.

"Well, it's about time you admitted that." Jimmy smirked and put both hands behind his head, propping his feet on the desk in front of him.

Hot tears fell uncontrollably down my cheeks as I ran out the classroom door. My feet carried me down the hall, and I ran as fast as I could, needing to get out of the building, to go somewhere safe so Taylor and I could talk this through. If I knew my best friend, I was sure he would know where to find me.

Chapter Eleven—Taylor
She Loves You, She Loves You Not

"What the flipping nightmare is this?" I held up the newspaper in shock. Right there in black and white on the front page was my brother and my best friend practically kissing and holding hands.

How could he? He knows how I feel about her!

Or does he? Hmm… I've called her my best friend so many times it's as if I'm trying to convince myself. But is that the truth? No, she's way more than a best friend.

Kade hurried around the corner into homeroom, holding the newspaper.

I took a step back. "Don't you even have the nerve to talk to me!"

"Tay, none of it is true!" Kade said. "You have to believe me!"

"You have ruined my life over and over. I shouldn't be surprised that you would do this to me after you *promised* you would never ruin my life again. I don't know why I ever trusted you."

"Tay, that's harsh. You know darn well that I never intended for her to fall in love with me. Heck, I know she's *not* in love with me because she's in love with you!"

"She doesn't even like me that way," I insisted.

"And she's obviously in love with you. The pictures don't lie."

"See that picture right there." Kade pointed to the picture of him kissing Gracie's forehead. I wanted to puke. "I had just told her that *you* were lucky to have her because I knew from talking to her, and from being your brother, that you were in love with each other."

I hoped no one in my homeroom caught that he called himself my brother, but I was past caring. "I may be in love with her, but I *know* she doesn't like me that way."

"Actually, she does." Dean, one of our friends in homeroom, held up his cell phone with an Instagram post about Gracie running from her homeroom, crying after admitting that the reason she *wasn't* in love with Kade was because she *was* in love with Tay.

"What?" I grabbed his cell phone in disbelief. "I thought she didn't like me that way."

"That is your own denial, my brother." There he goes again, calling himself my brother. That rumor was going to get back to Gracie too. Oh well. "She loves you, and you love her, and you guys need to just admit that to each other. Because you've admitted it to us, and she's admitted it to her friends. It's time you two talk to one another."

"I don't even know where she is," I said, dejected. "She ran away and who knows where she went."

"Well, you know her better than anybody else," Kade said. "Where do you think she went?"

61

Immediately, I knew she went to our secret spot. I didn't even bother saying goodbye to my friends or explaining myself to our teacher. I grabbed my book bag and ran from the room.

Chapter Twelve—Gracie
Our Little Secret

To the south of the baseball diamonds there were several wooded acres. Taylor and I had wandered this way while trying to find an adventurous way home after a football game our junior year. Instead, we came across a weeping willow tree at the corner of the school's property where a fence blocked our progression.

Neither of us were ready to go home for the night, so we built a little fort under that tree, and we declared it our secret spot. Whenever we needed to get away from the world for a while, we came here.

I ran the entire way to the woods then plopped myself down at the base of our tree and sobbed into my knees. I didn't care that the ground was still wet with this morning's dew nor that it would ruin my capri pants.

Although I was missing French class, my teacher, Ms. Moreau, was extremely forgiving. I would probably be hiding in her classroom during lunch, anyway, crying about this morning's drama. There was no way I could confront anyone before talking with Taylor about what happened.

I heard twigs snap, and I peeked over my knees to see Taylor standing in front of me. I couldn't bring myself to look him in the eye. I didn't want to see the hurt that he must have felt after seeing those pictures of me with his cousin.

He stood there for what seemed like an eternity but was really only a few seconds, saying nothing while I cried.

"I'm sorry, Tay." I looked up at him with my tear-streaked face. "Those pictures aren't real. I mean they're real, but they were taken completely out of context."

"Hey now." Taylor crouched in front of me and placed a hand on top of mine where they clutched my knees tight to my chest. "It's okay."

"How can you say that?" I questioned as I glanced up at him. His cologne mixed with the fresh spring breeze comforted me, but I couldn't maintain eye contact, so I returned to burying my face in my knees and said in a muffled voice, "Everyone thinks I'm in love with Kade, but I'm not."

"I'm pretty sure almost no one thinks you're in love with Kade," Taylor reassured me. "It wouldn't be the first time something was wrong in the school paper, right?"

That was true, but it didn't change how I felt about the situation. "Jimmy was a huge jerk and kept saying awful things about me."

"Jimmy's always been a jerk," Taylor said. "That's one of the reasons I encouraged you to break up with him."

"One of the reasons?" I asked sheepishly as I peered

over my knees, to see Taylor looking at me with soft intensity.

"Gracie, I haven't been honest with you," Taylor said softly.

"About what?" I asked, no longer trying to hide my tears. Taylor reached out and wiped them away from my eyes. He took a deep breath, then looked up to meet my gaze.

"About my feelings. I've been in love with you since we met."

"You have?" Was I surprised? No, not really. Suspected? Yeah, probably.

"You're so unlike anyone I've ever met. Instead of wallowing in self-pity when your parents are fighting, you played tennis." Taylor continued. You're authentic and honest, and you don't try to hide anything about yourself. You're kind, brave, funny, beautiful."

Now he was just making me self-conscious. I could never live up to his vision of perfection.

With a furrowed brow, he took another deep breath and gently held both of my hands in his. Letting out a nervous chuckle accompanied by a crooked smile, he shyly continued. "Gracie, you're everything I've ever wanted. You mean the world to me. More than you'll ever know. I love you."

Taylor helped me up from the ground. Placing one hand on the small of my back, he pulled me close so our bodies were touching. With his other hand, he cradled my cheek and turned my face up to look him in the eye. His warmth drew me in closer as I instinctively wrapped my arms around his waist. My heart raced, and I got lost in his deep brown eyes.

He pulled my face to his, and our lips met as the world stopped moving. Nothing in my life had ever felt this right. I clenched his jacket with my hands and pulled him closer to me, kissing him with the longing that I'd been suppressing for nearly two years.

Everything in that single moment was perfect and how it should be. I loved Taylor Kendrick and had since meeting him on the tennis court two summers ago.

As he pulled away, we were both breathing heavily, and he placed his forehead on mine. I kept my eyes closed, not wanting this moment to end.

"I love you too, Tay," I whispered, opening my eyes to see a smile on his face.

"I've dreamed of hearing you say those words," Taylor said.

We pulled each other back in for another kiss, but not nearly as long this time. Ending the kiss with a sigh, we embraced one another, prolonging the moment now that we'd admitted the truth.

"I think it's time to head back," Taylor said softly.

"Already?" I protested with a suggestive pout.

Taylor tucked a lock of my hair behind my ear, and I leaned into his hand as he stroked my cheek with his thumb. "I think we've missed enough of our French class already."

I sighed. "You're probably right. At least Ms. Moreau is understanding."

"And I'm sure she would love to hear about your traumatic morning," Taylor said, knowing I frequently confided in Ms. Moreau. "But maybe don't tell her we were making out in the woods, hmm? We don't want our parents to get a call from the school." He leaned down and placed one quick kiss on the tip of my nose.

"I won't kiss and tell." I bit my lower lip, already wanting to kiss him again.

When Taylor released me from his embrace, I shivered in the cool morning air. He took off his jacket and wrapped it around my shoulders, then wrapped his arm around my waist, guiding me in the direction of the school.

As we left our secret place in the woods, I never wanted this feeling to go away. Everything was going to be different now. Taylor and I could be together as boyfriend and girlfriend. My Taylor.

Chapter Thirteen—Taylor
An Escort to Chemistry

We missed French class. Well, we missed the *class* part. I couldn't believe my luck. My heart raced as we walked into the school amid taunts from my friends. Not trying to hide my grin, I welcomed their catcalls and whistles as I, finally, walked my girlfriend to her locker. That was going to take some getting used to.

My girlfriend. Gracie Hansen is my girlfriend. I wanted to shout it from the bleachers. But I really didn't need to shout because everyone could see my arm around Gracie. My girlfriend.

My twin brother waited for us beside Gracie's locker, with a smirk on his face. "Looks like you no longer need me to walk you to class, gorgeous, I mean, Gracie."

"No, I think I can take it from here, Kade," I said with confidence.

"Very funny, you two." Gracie slipped from my arms to reach for her locker combination.

I felt her absence and missed her warmth. Like a welcome security blanket, one of my hoodies was hanging in her locker, and I reached over her to grab it.

"Do you want your jacket back," she asked, the innocent apprehension in her expression begging me not to ask for the jacket.

"Nah, you can wear it for the rest of the day." I slipped the hoodie over my head and relished the way her perfume clung to every fiber. She'd borrowed the sweatshirt a long time ago, and I decided I'd never wash it again.

"So, does this mean I can't take you to prom next week?" Kade asked with a purposely innocent expression.

"Don't go there, dude."

"Mind if I ask Maddie to go with me?" Kade asked Gracie. "She's in my band class. Her voice in smoking hot."

"Oh my gosh, she would *love* that." Gracie bounced on her toes with excitement. "We can double date again."

"Only if my boutonniere matches your corsage," I said. "I don't want anyone to question which one of us you're in love with this time."

"Never again." Gracie leaned closer and lifted onto her toes to touch her lips to mine.

"Blech," Kade said with a gagging sound. "You can find your own escort to chemistry class. I'm out of here." He pushed away from the lockers and started down the hall.

I ignored my brother for a few seconds as I got lost in Gracie's kiss, savoring the moment without pushing our luck. No need to get called out for public display of affection on our first day as an official couple. Pulling back just a little I asked, "Could I walk you to chemistry class from now on?"

"That would be awesome." As she stepped away from me, she ran right into her old friend-turned-enemy, Laura Miller. Gracie didn't flinch away from the girl who had caused us so much trouble that morning. Instead, she got right in Laura's face. The sound that emerged from deep inside her was almost a growl. "How could you?"

Chapter Fourteen—Gracie
Confronting Laura

When Laura didn't answer me, I asked again, slower and with more anger. "How... could... you?"

"I'm not sure what you mean," Laura said with a furrowed brow and pursed lips.

"You know what I mean, Laura," I snapped with obvious aggression. "Why would you make up all of those blatant lies and then put it on the front page of the school paper?"

Laura shrugged and stuck her nose higher as she said, "What? I'm just an effective journalist."

I didn't even try to hold back my anger. "You know darn well that that is not journalism. That is gossip-column mediocrity. Now the entire school knows that you lied."

"Do they, though?" Laura asked rhetorically.

I looked around to see our classmates videoing us on their phones. Why is everyone so interested in my love life?

"Yes, they do," Taylor said as he stepped next to me, putting his arm around my shoulders and pulling me close to himself. I relaxed a little, being in his arms and taking in his cologne, but my emotions were still burning with fire.

"I'm not so sure everyone is convinced," Laura said

snarkily. "I may have added a few extra juicy details for flare, but those pictures are very much real, and so is your relationship with Kade."

"I am not in love with Kade," I said through clenched teeth.

"Gracie, you've told me so many times that you weren't in love with Tay either," Laura said. She looked at him out of the corner of her eye with what looked like a loathsome glare. "Yet, here you stand. So graciously wrapped around each other. Like two love-sick puppies finally being honest for the first time in two years."

Taylor flinched, and I could tell that Laura was starting to get to him.

"Tay and I are honest with each other," I said. "We don't keep secrets from each other."

"Like being in love with each other?" Laura asked.

"If I could interject here," Taylor said, clearing his throat. "I think we both knew deep down we were in love with each other, but we didn't want to ruin our friendship. That wasn't being dishonest. More like in denial."

"Oh really, Tay? Do you *really* want to talk about being dishonest?" Laura smirked, her sarcasm implying she knew something else he was lying about. Up to this point, her journalism bunny trails had led toward catastrophe, so I decided to take it with a grain of salt because I didn't want to be anywhere near that drama bomb.

Taylor shoved his free hand into his pocket and looked at his feet, showing that he was giving up this fight that really wasn't even worth having, but unlike my chivalrous boyfriend, I wasn't going down that easy.

"Yes, Laura," I said. "He is always honest with me. Like, what is your problem? Why did you start hating me the second he showed up?"

Laura looked me square in the eye and rhetorically asked in a shallow voice, "You really have no idea, do you?"

She turned and started to walk away from me, but I followed her down the hall. I grabbed her shoulder and pulled her back around so we were standing face to face, our noses nearly touching.

"No," I said. "You don't get to just walk away from me. We are having this conversation. Right here. Right now."

"You know what Gracie?" Laura narrowed her eyes at me. "The world doesn't revolve around you. I don't have to do a thing you say because I'm not your little assistant just waiting at your beck and call."

"You were never an assistant, Laura," I said with animosity.

"Oh yeah, who was the one you called when your parents were fighting?" Laura asked.

"That isn't fair, that is just being a good frie—" I said before Laura interjected and continued on.

"Who was the one who crawled through your

window at night when you needed a friend to talk to?"

I stood there, not knowing how to respond to the girl who used to be my best friend.

Laura continued. "Who was the one who brought you your favorite snack every Friday for lunch since Kindergarten? Who was the one who took you on every family fourth of July camping trip since sixth grade? Who was the one who came over when your dog of ten years died? Who was the one who introduced you to your beloved tennis? Who was the one who bought you your first racket for your twelfth birthday with all of her babysitting money? Who was the one who let you cry on their shoulder anytime any little, tiny, bad thing happened in your life? Who was the one, Gracie?"

I continued to stand there, and I wanted to say something, but I still couldn't find the words.

"Because it sure wasn't him," Laura stated, pointing at Taylor, but still looking me square in the eyes. "And I am no longer your doormat."

Without even giving me a second glance, Laura turned on her heels and walked away from me. I wanted to chase after her and tell her I'm sorry, but I didn't think it would do any good. I wanted to tell her that she meant so much to me even now, but I knew it would fall on deaf ears. She had loved me like a sister once, and now she knew me as her enemy, and that stung.

Taylor and I might be best friends now, but Laura and I went back to childhood best friends. We had been friends since we were five years old. A part of me will always be with Laura, and nothing was ever going to be able to change the time we spent together.

Tears pricked my eyes as part of my heart began to grieve, perhaps for the first time, the friend that I once had, realizing that I will most likely never be able to have that friendship again.

The day had been melancholy and bittersweet. On one hand, I was finally with the guy I had been in love with for two years, but on the other, I had been embarrassed beyond imagination and had gotten raked over the coals by my ex-best friend.

And it was only Monday morning.

Chapter Fifteen Taylor—Gracie Madison Square Garden

I can't wait to see you in your prom dress, I texted my new girlfriend. That was still fun to say. Gracie and Maddie planned to come to our house when they were done primping. Kade and I were helping babysit our little sister until then.

School gave us Friday off. They said it was for a professional development day, but we really knew that it was for prom.

Kade and I both had changed into our tuxes, minus the jackets, which we'd draped over the backs of chairs in the dining room.

See you in a couple of hours. I'm excited to see your tux, Gracie texted back, with a winking emoji.

I put the phone down, turned back to the Disney movie, and laughed for another two hours with my siblings. I was surprised the time had gone by so quickly when Gracie and Maddie walked in the back door.

"Gracie!" Reina pushed herself off my lap and scrambled to get down from the couch. She raced across the room and jumped into Gracie's arms. Thankfully, her Elsa costume didn't rip with that jump either. To her credit, Gracie didn't flinch about Reina messing up her evening gown. "You look like a princess, Gracie." Reina couldn't help herself from oohing and aahing, and I couldn't take my eyes off of her either.

"Thanks," Gracie said. "So do you." She tickled Reina.

"Come watch Frozen with us."

"How many times have you seen that movie?" Gracie asked, stepping around Clay, who was lying in the middle of the living room floor. She waved Maddie to follow her and sat beside me on the couch.

Kade rose from his chair to welcome Maddie over to the other end of the sectional, and sat beside her as they chatted about music and their makeshift band.

"Wow. Gracie, you look amazing," I said, sneaking her a quick kiss when Reina had her head turned. We had spent nearly every second together since making our relationship official. Part of it was to avoid any rumors or drama that were circling from the paper fiasco on Monday. The other part was because I just couldn't keep my hands off of her after waiting two long years.

"You don't look so bad yourself." Gracie tucked a stray lock of hair behind her ear and lowered her eyes. I wished all these people weren't in here with us so I could pull her close. "How are you?"

"Good. Are you excited for our date?" I wished we could leave now, but we were waiting for our mom to get home from visiting our dad. She would kill us if we left before she had a chance to take pictures of us in our dresses and tuxes.

"Where are you going on a date?" Reina asked, turning to Gracie.

"We are going to prom," Gracie answered, pulling on Reina's ponytail.

"Can I come with you? Pleeeeease?" Reina knew how to turn up the charm.

"Not this time." Gracie turned Reina around so she was facing forward. "Do you want me to braid your hair?" Good distraction.

"Yes!" Reina climbed down and ran to the bathroom. She came back with her comb and detangling spray and stood in front of Gracie, leaning her head back and looking up at the ceiling.

"Dang, you have a lot of snarls. Didn't your mommy do your hair before bed last night?"

"She's still gone visiting Daddy," Reina said, her eyes now focused on the television.

Gracie looked over at me with raised eyebrows. "I thought your parents were divorced."

Oh boy, here we go. "I've never actually said that. You just assumed."

"But… you go and visit your dad's house only during school breaks. Aren't your parents separated?"

"Uh… no, not officially."

"Why didn't you go with your mom to visit your dad?"

"They are bunny rabbits," Reina said. "None of my brothers want to be in the same wing of the house because they don't want to think about what Mommy and Daddy are doing. I don't know what that means."

Maddie snickered, and Gracie openly laughed.

"Kids say the darndest things," I said, chuckling along with the girls as if I wasn't dreading the rest of this conversation.

"She's just saying what the rest of us are thinking," Clay said, rolling onto his back and tucking his hands behind his head. No one seemed to be paying any attention to the Disney movie anymore.

"What did you mean by the same wing of the house?" Maddie asked.

"Our big house has wings." Reina flapped her arms like a bird. "Our little house doesn't have any wings."

I held my breath, hoping Gracie didn't ask. She did. "How many houses do you have?"

"We have three houses," Reina said without turning from where Gracie was still combing through tangles. "A big house, a little house, and a house near grandma and grandpa in England. We have to fly in an airplane to get to that house."

"Wait… this is your *little* house?" Maddie asked, glancing up at the cathedral ceiling, the 72" television mounted on the wall, and the imported furniture.

"I have two bedrooms at my daddy's house." Reina turned around and held up two fingers. "They call one of them my playroom because there are lots of toys. But I like Clay's playroom better because he has lots of video games and bean bags. I'm not allowed to go into

Kade's playroom because there are too many guitars in there. And he has a *whole* drum set right in his playroom. It's not as big as Uncle Nathan's drum set. But that's downstairs in the studio. I'm not allowed to go down there without Daddy or Mommy."

I held my head in my hands, gripping my hair.

"Well, I guess that cat's outta the bag." Kade snickered.

"Dude, this isn't funny." I lifted my head and glared across the room where my twin brother leaned back into the sofa beside his date.

"We only have six bedrooms in this house." Reina continued her speech that was destroying my perfect little world. "And they're all crammed together on one floor."

"How many bedrooms are in your big house?" Gracie asked through clenched teeth, glaring at me. I was in so much trouble.

"I don't know. A whole bunch of them." Reina shrugged.

"Fifteen," Clay said without lifting his head.

"Fifteen?" Maddie's question was practically a squeal. "How come you don't live in your big house?"

"We came to live here after Grandma Kendrick had her heart attack." That was our standard answer as a family. Reina was repeating the narrative she'd been taught. Maybe Gracie would accept that and move on with our evening.

"If your mommy is visiting your daddy at his big house, why aren't you visiting also?" Gracie was getting more out of this conversation with my little sister in five minutes than I'd told her in the two years I'd been her next-door neighbor and best friend. Might as well let this train wreck happen so we can finally get it over with. I knew what was coming next, and I cringed.

"Daddy's on tour," Reina said. "They're at a hotel somewhere in New York City. They played in a garden last night."

"A garden?" Maddie asked. "Do you mean Central Park?"

"No, it was a square garden," Reina said.

"*Madison* Square Garden?" Gracie's jaw dropped, and I saw the moment she connected the last dots that had been right in front of her eyes for so long she was probably embarrassed this had taken her so long to figure out. "Your dad is Kai Burton."

"How did you know my daddy's name?" Reina asked, turning around and looking at Gracie with big eyes.

Gracie looked back and forth between me and Clay. Kade turned his head away, tracing the pattern on the arm of the sofa. "Oh my gosh, you look just like him. I can't believe I never…"

"Sorry," I whispered.

"Why haven't you ever told me who your father was?" Gracie sounded as if she was going to cry.

"Wait, are you talking about Kai Burton, the lead guitarist of the rock band Buxton Peak?" Maddie finally connected her own set of dots.

"Please understand our perspective here." I ignored Maddie and spoke directly to Gracie. "We just want to lead a normal life without all the fame and stuff."

"By lying about who you were?" Gracie asked.

"We didn't lie... we just didn't tell the whole truth."

"Same thing."

"Maybe you guys should talk about this another time," Clay said. He reached over to pick up Reina, who now had perfect little braids on either side of her head. "How about if I feed Reina her bedtime snack, and you four can head out on your date? Sounds like you have lots to talk about when little ears aren't around."

"Great idea." Gracie stood and folded her arms across her chest. "We do have lots to talk about."

"Alright, let's do this." Kade hopped up from the sofa, offered his hand to Maddie and lifted her to stand beside him. He looked directly at me and said, "The truth will finally set us free."

"The truth," I mumbled. Wait until she finds out the rest of the truth. I had an ominous feeling that this was going to be the worst night of my life.

Chapter Sixteen—Gracie
Now You Know (Some of) the Truth

"I cannot believe you lied to me," I grumbled, clicking my high-heeled shoes on the kitchen's expensive tile floor as I headed out to the car. "What else are you lying about?"

"A whole buncha stuff," Kade said from behind us.

"Shut up, Kade!" Taylor demanded, turning around and glaring at his cousin.

"A whole buncha stuff, huh?" I stopped near the doorway of the mudroom and glared at Taylor.

"Don't listen to him." Taylor put his arm around me and guided me out the door and toward his BMW. "Let's go to prom and have a good time, okay?"

"Shouldn't we at least talk about your dad being Kai freaking Burton?" I didn't even try to hide my frustration of him lying about his family for the past two years.

Just as we were leaving the house, Taylor's mom's car pulled in the driveway and she hurried to exit her vehicle. "Did I miss getting pictures?"

"We're still here," Taylor grumbled then asked me, "Do you want to ask your mom to come out and get pictures too?"

Without answering him I took out my phone, feeling silly for calling my mom from next door. "Hey Mom, do you and Dad want to come out and get pictures before we leave for prom?"

"Oh, wait, I almost forgot. I'll be right back." Taylor left me standing there holding my phone and headed into the house. He came out with a small box tied with a gold bow. Looped through the ribbon was a rose charm for my bracelet. "That's so we can remember our prom together."

I pulled the ribbon away and opened the box to reveal an elegant corsage and matching boutonniere. They each had a single red rose accented by small blush pink budding peonies, all held together with black ribbon and sparkling crystals. These weren't the average corsage and boutonniere combo sold at the local flower shop. "Oh, Tay, they're beautiful."

"Ooh, let me get pictures of you putting her corsage on," Taylor's mom said with excitement.

"May I?" Taylor lifted the corsage from its box and slid it onto my wrist. The red and soft pink complemented my black satin dress.

Taylor lifted my hand to his lips and kissed it. "I love you, Gracie."

"I love you too," I said with a small smile, then lowered my brows. "We still have a lot to talk about."

"Yeah, let's uh… talk in the car."

"Okay, now one of Gracie pinning your boutonniere onto your lapel," his mom said.

I lifted the boutonniere and carefully pinned it to his tailored black tux.

We spent the next ten minutes patiently moving throughout our two yards, allowing our parents to pose us in all the desired locations. On Taylor's front porch steps, on my back patio, near the flowering Magnolia tree in Taylor's backyard. Throughout the whole ordeal, we all smiled fake smiles and pretended there wasn't this huge secret hanging over us.

"We'll meet you guys there," I said to Maddie, who took the hint that she and Kade should drive separately.

"Sure thing." Maddie nodded, then turned to Kade. "This is your lucky night. You get to ride in my girl Ethel. My grandad restored this beauty when I was a little girl, and now it's all mine." Maddie pointed at her Grandpa's 1966 black Mustang convertible.

"Whoa!" Kade exclaimed. "This baby is sweet." Kade jogged over to Maddie's car, inspecting it as if he knew something about cars. Maybe he did, or maybe he was just admiring it. How would I know since I've been lied to already about how they're related to a famous rock star.

"Ready to go?" Taylor asked in a soft voice. Taylor opened the passenger door for me. His nervous stutter was understandable, considering how mad I was for him lying to me.

I could see the remorse in his eyes. I knew he loved me, and I loved him too, but I was still mad that he lied. I climbed into the passenger seat as Taylor rounded the front of the car, climbed into the driver's side, and turned the key in the ignition.

As we backed out of the driveway, he asked, "So,

what do you want to know?"

"Well, first, why didn't you tell me who your dad was?"

"I didn't want to be known as the son of a famous rock star. I didn't want to be known as someone who had a lot of money because of who his dad was. I wanted to be known just for being me."

"Okay, that's fair," I said. "But why wouldn't you tell me after we had been friends for so long?"

"I guess I just didn't want our friendship to change, and I was worried you would treat me differently if you knew who my dad was."

"Tay, you know me better than that."

"Yeah, that's true," Tay said. "I guess another reason is because I've gotten used to it just being my mom and siblings, then you and the tennis team, and I just liked how life finally felt normal. You know?"

"Well, I can't know for sure since I'm not related to an incredibly rich rock star. But I can kind of see where you're coming from."

"Now you know why I'm such a Buxton Peak fan."

I laughed. "Yeah, I was just rolling with your obsession because it made you happy."

"See, that is one of the many reasons I love you."

I smiled, but then remembered why I was still angry. "Kade said there was a whole buncha stuff you were lying about. What else?"

Taylor was silent for a moment, then sighed. "A few

years ago, Kade did some things to me and my family that were awful to say the least, and I'm having a hard time forgiving him. I'm actually surprised he wants you to know about our argument."

"Well, maybe that's a sign that he's changed."

Taylor grumbled. "I'm not convinced he's changed."

"Has he given you any reason to suggest he hasn't?" I asked.

Taylor seemed to contemplate for a moment. "No, but I still don't trust him."

"Well, it seems to me that you are the only one still hurting from all of that."

"Yeah, it seems that way," Taylor grumbled again.

"Why do you think that is?"

"Because he has everyone else wrapped around his little finger."

"Perhaps. Or maybe it's because he actually has changed, and everyone else sees that, but you're so caught up in how he wronged you that you won't even give him a chance to be forgiven and hear things from his perspective."

"You're probably right." Taylor let out a long sigh. I squeezed his hand to show that I was supporting him.

We arrived at the event center, and Taylor put the car in park. We both sat there, not moving. I wasn't quite done with this conversation, and Taylor seemed to respect that. "Can you promise me two things?" I asked, breaking the silence.

"Definitely." Taylor nodded and looked over at me.

"One, can you try to be friends with your cousin again?" I asked. "From what he's told me, you guys used to be really close. I think he misses you a lot."

Taylor raised his eyebrows, then cleared his throat. "I'll try. What's the second thing?"

"I want you to promise that you won't lie to me again. About anything. We need to be honest with each other if we want this relationship to work, which I do. I wouldn't want to be dating a liar, let alone be friends with one."

"Gracie, I do want our relationship to work. But there are things I've been hiding from you for years, and I'm sorry." Taylor gulped and took a deep breath. "I promise not to lie to you again. But promise that you'll forgive me as you learn about my past."

"Of course, I'll forgive you." I leaned over the center console, and he met me halfway for a sweet kiss, at least it started that way. Taylor wrapped his hand around the nape of my neck, low enough that I wasn't worried about my updo. He didn't seem to be holding back his passion. I gripped my hands into his hair, pulling him closer.

We were interrupted by a knock on our windows and pulled away from each other to find Kade and Maddie standing outside the car.

"Are you lovebirds ready to go?" Kade asked with a smirk.

"Not really," Taylor grumbled as he climbed out of

the car. He shut the door and pulled Kade aside. I couldn't hear what they were saying, but I hoped Taylor was offering Kade forgiveness and renewed friendship.

Maddie stepped aside as I opened my door. "You okay, girl?" She draped her arm through mine as we walked into the event center, our dates trailing behind us, still deep in conversation.

I wanted to let them have this moment and turned my attention to Maddie. "Yeah, I'm good. How was your ride over here?"

"Oh, it was fantastic!" Maddie didn't even try to contain her excitement. "Did you know that Kade has been learning to play the guitar since he was six years old? His dad wanted to be sure he was a great player, and it came as no surprise that he was naturally talented at it."

"Really?" I asked. "I didn't know he'd started playing that young. I've heard him play, and he's definitely talented."

I was still a little off emotionally since finding out Taylor had lied to me. I forgave him, but it didn't change the fact that it hurt. Hopefully a prom full of fun, food, and dancing would be just the thing to take my mind off the drama and enjoy time with my best friend, who also happened to now be my boyfriend.

As Taylor and Kade hurried around us to open the doors, I decided to make this the best night of our lives.

Chapter Seventeen—Taylor—Twins

"Oh, aren't you guys cute with your matching corsage and boutonniere," Laura Miller said, stalking toward us in the foyer of the event center where prom was barely underway. I instinctively took a step between my date and this former friend who seemed to have a bone to pick with Gracie. "I would have thought that the *identical twins* would want to wear something that matched."

"We are not *identical* twins," Kade told Laura. "We're fraternal twins."

"Shut up, Kade!" I demanded, already knowing it was too late.

"What? Don't you think it's time Gracie learned the truth? She knows about Dad. Time to tell her about us."

"What are you guys talking about?" Gracie asked.

"Oh, come on, Gracie." Kade turned to her. "You nailed it the first time you saw us standing next to each other. I don't know why Tay thought he could pass me off as his cousin. We may be fraternal twins, but we look identical. Admit it."

"Oh my gosh." Gracie looked back and forth between us. "You do look identical."

"Well, we're not." I glared at Kade. "I'm nothing like him. We have zero in common."

"Other than our birthdates and our love for Buxton Peak," Kade said, not backing down. "I still can't believe she didn't figure it out the night of our date to the mini-golf putting thing."

"You were lying to me this whole time?" Gracie was no longer focused on Kade. She had narrowed eyes shooting proverbial daggers at me. "You purposely made up a story telling everyone he was your cousin? Why?"

"Because I didn't want him ruining my life again." I tried to justify my reasoning.

"Oh, grow up, Tay," Kade said. "You don't even know the full story of what I did."

"And you"—Gracie turned on Kade— "You went along with Tay's scheme, and you even pretended you liked me."

"I did like you," Kade said. "I *do* like you. You're a great person."

"Yeah, I'm such a good person that you both thought it was okay to lie to me."

Gracie ripped the corsage off her wrist and whipped it in our direction. Kade caught the corsage and handed it to me.

"I wish you had never come here, Kade! What Tay and I had was perfect, and now it's like the Tay I thought I knew is gone!"

Kade was silent. He looked down at his feet, and Maddie wrapped her arm around his waist.

91

Gracie turned on me again. "You said you loved me and that you would never lie to me. You promised me a few minutes ago you would never lie to me again."

"I haven't lied to you again," I defended. "And you promised that you'd forgive me as you learn about my past."

"I gave you the chance to tell me everything. How could you still not trust me enough to tell me the truth?"

I reached out to her, trying to hold on to the small thread of hope that she would hear my reasoning. "Gracie, please…"

She stepped back, holding out her hands so that I couldn't get close enough to touch her. Tears streamed down her cheeks.

"You lied to me." She looked back and forth between me and Kade.

"Well, to be fair," Kade said, "I was just doing as I was asked." His argument was not helping my defense.

Gracie glared at me. "So you told him to lie to me?"

"Gracie, it isn't like that," I said.

"It's exactly like that, Tay," Gracie said. "I cannot believe it took me this long to see it. I'm such a fool." She turned on her heels, beelining towards the ladies' room, the one place I couldn't follow her.

"Why did you do that?" I took a step toward Laura, my fists balled at my side.

"Whoa, whoa, whoa, Scrappy," Kade said. "As your one and only twin brother, it is my responsibility to keep you from going to jail for hitting a girl at prom."

"Gracie deserved to know the truth about you," Laura said with a smirk. "She deserved to know what kind of guy she abandoned me for."

"Abandoned you?" Maddie asked. "You're the one who quit the tennis team and stopped answering her calls. You're the one who abandoned her."

"She abandoned me long before I quit," Laura said. "She abandoned me the minute Tay moved into our neighborhood. She immediately started calling him her best friend, as if she didn't already have a best friend."

"Gracie has lots of best friends," Maddie said. "And she never understood why you no longer wanted to be one of them."

"Well, maybe I should go talk to her." Laura backed away from us. "Since her *boy*friend is not allowed in the ladies' room." Laura turned on her strappy high-heeled shoes. Her violet prom dress swished as she walked away.

Chapter Eighteen—Gracie
You Deserve the Truth

The ladies' room in the event center had a nice powder area, and I plopped myself on the striped couch directly across from the massive wall-to-wall mirror. I didn't want to cry and mess up my makeup. Maddie had worked on my face for over an hour. I grabbed a tissue from the end table next to me to pat my eyes.

Taylor and Kade were twins. It was undeniable. As the dots connected in front of me, disbelief clouded my thoughts. How could I not have seen this before?

I didn't understand why Taylor would lie to me. I gave him the opportunity not even ten minutes prior to tell me the complete truth, but he still chose to withhold information from me.

The mirror stared back. I was pathetic, sitting here in my black satin gown, glitzy jewelry, and red eyes from the tears fighting to fall down my cheeks. I fought back and dabbed at my eyes again.

"Really, Gracie?" I grumbled at my reflection. "Were you really this blind to Tay's lies? Son of a rock star, probably a millionaire, twin to someone who didn't exist until two weeks ago? You're pathetic."

"Maybe just a little," Laura said, standing by the door to the ladies' room. When did she come in? How much had she heard of my ramblings? Great.

"Don't you have someone else to patronize?" I asked, rolling my eyes and looking back toward my reflection.

"You know you deserve better than that, right Gracie?" Laura said in a kind voice.

I glanced over at her, perplexed. Why was she being nice to me? "Everything was perfect before Kade got here." There, I'd said it out loud. Granted, I said it to the girl who used to be my best friend, but whatever. "I mean, yeah, I was hiding my feelings from Tay. But people were nice to me, and I certainly had a lot less drama."

"Gracie, you've always had drama," Laura said, clicking her tongue and laughing softly. There she goes, patronizing me again. I half-wondered if she was going to pat me on the head as she walked past and sat next to me on the sofa.

I furrowed my eyebrows and turned to face her. "What do you mean by that?"

Laura folded her hands and placed them on her violet satin gown. "Oh, come on, Gracie. You used to call me almost every night with the same whining. 'My parents are fighting. I don't know if I'm good enough for tennis. So-and-so doesn't like me.' It was exhausting to say the least."

I was offended but had to admit she was right. I hadn't meant to be whiny and needy. "I guess it makes sense why you didn't want to be my friend anymore."

"Yeah, that would make sense." Laura glanced down at her perfectly manicured hands, and she took another deep breath. "But that wasn't why I stopped being your friend."

Her words were so quiet I wasn't sure if she'd meant to say them out loud. I heard it though, and I couldn't ignore it. "So why *did* you stop being my friend?"

Laura closed her eyes, and her leg bounced as it did when she was nervous.

"It's okay, Laura," I encouraged. "I won't be mad. I want to know so I can make it right. You deserve that."

Laura turned to look at me. "I couldn't be your friend anymore after I saw you with Tay," she said. "It was like he replaced me, and that hurt, especially after we had been friends for so long."

I could tell that there was more she wanted to tell me, so I sat there until she was ready to talk.

Laura took another deep breath and let it out slowly. She clutched the skirt of her satin prom dress with her fists, opening and closing her hands as if she were kneading a stress ball. I could tell that whatever she was about to say was the real reason she was no longer my friend. I held my breath, suspecting I already knew the truth.

"Haven't you done enough damage?" Maddie said from the doorway, interrupting the first time Laura and I had talked in several years.

Laura stood and took a step back, that same mask of anger once again on her face.

"Maddie, it's okay," I started to say.

"No, it's fine," Laura said to me. "You hang out with your other best friend, and I'll talk to you another time." Laura gave Maddie a wide berth as she skirted around Maddie to get to the door. And then she was gone, taking with her the real reason why she'd stopped being my friend.

Chapter Nineteen—Taylor
The Whole Truth

"You purposely told Gracie about us being twins after I specifically forbid you from doing that." I glared at my brother, my fisted hands twitching to show him just how angry I was.

"How long were you planning to keep that up?" Kade stepped right up into my face, almost begging me to throw the first punch. "You were just prolonging the inevitable. The longer that lie went on, the worse the ramifications."

"I wanted to keep it up through graduation and then move away from you for good so you couldn't ruin my life again. Although I'm sure you would have found a way."

"You're such a jerk, Tay." Kade pointed in my face. "I don't know why I even try with you. Twin brothers or not, I'm done trying to be perfect for you. You can't see my side of anything. You made me lie for you. You won't trust me that I can stay clean."

"This isn't about the drugs," I said, aware that we'd drawn a captive audience in the foyer outside the ballroom. Prom was happening without us. "I can't forgive you for what you did."

"What did he do?" Gracie asked from behind me. I spun around to find that my angry girlfriend and Maddie had snuck up behind me while I was yelling at my brother.

"Shall I list all the reasons he went to juvie?" I asked with disdain. "Using drugs, dealing drugs, theft, breaking and entering. Am I missing anything, Kade?"

"I have been sober for two years, and I've done my time for everything else," Kade said.

"You've only been sober because you were locked up, admit it." I sneered at Kade. "And you deserve a lot more time for what you did."

"You don't even know what I did," Kade shouted in my face. "I took the fall for everyone else that night. The only reason I went back into the house was to return your PRS."

"What?" I glared at my brother. "You were *stealing* my guitar. You were caught with it in your arms."

"Because I was returning it."

"No, you were stealing that with everything else you tried stealing. And because of that choice, we had to uproot everything and come here, missing the life we'd built in Nashville."

"Tay," Kade said, "I'm sorry you were forced to move away, but that was Mom's choice, and it was a long time coming. As for the guitar, my friends were the ones trying to steal it. I was just barely sober enough to know not to let them get away with your guitar."

"Why didn't you ever tell me that?" I took a step back, feeling as if someone had shoved me in the chest.

"Would you have even listened? I was so flippin' stoned I didn't know what I was saying to anyone. I was trying to explain, but nothing was coming out right. They had to take me to detox before they could take me to jail. It was not a fun night for me."

"Well, you shouldn't have been doing drugs." I was still angry even after everything he'd confessed.

"I know that now," Kade said. "And I never will again. I promise. If Andy can stay sober after all these years, I know I can."

"Who's Andy?" Maddie asked, slipping up beside Kade and sneaking her hand into his, probably to show solidarity and to help diffuse the situation.

"Andy Smith," I answered. "Bassist for Buxton Peak."

"He visited me every single month the whole time I was locked up, which was a heckuva lot more than you visited."

"Why'd he visit you so much?" Gracie asked, compassion in her voice. I wanted her to comfort me the way Maddie was comforting my brother. He hadn't lied to his date though.

"He's my sponsor. My accountability partner. Andy knows what it's like to fight an addiction to drugs." Kade's voice lowered to a near whisper. "He doesn't want what happened to Gary to happen to me."

Gracie reached over and held Kade's other hand. "That's not going to happen to you." My jealousy flared even though I knew she was just being nice.

"Who's Gary?" Maddie asked. "And what happened to him?"

"He couldn't stay sober," Kade said. "He wrapped his Bentley around a tree and…" Kade didn't need to finish his sentence for the rest of us to know what happened.

"Gary was the original drummer for Buxton Peak," I said. "If you listen to their earlier albums, that's who you'll hear. He was probably one of the most talented drummers ever. Drugs destroyed his life."

"Speaking of talent." Maddie sidled up next to Kade, who wrapped his arm around her shoulder. "Now I understand how you got so talented. Makes perfect sense now that I know you're Kai Burton's son. What was that like? Growing up with a famous dad?"

"It sucks," Kade and I said at the same time.

"Everyone knows your business," Kade said. "Everyone expects something from you."

"People want to be friends with you just because your dad's famous," I said. "Girls only flirt with you because your dad's a rock star."

Gracie released Kade's hand and stepped closer to me, wrapping her arms around my waist. "I'm glad I didn't know your dad was famous. I don't want you ever questioning why I love you."

I tucked her into my arms and kissed the top of her head just as Kade released Maddie from his arms and reached out to shake mine.

"Will you please forgive me now that you know the

truth?" The hurt in my twin brother's eyes conveyed his remorse. "I never should have gotten involved with drugs, and I never should have stolen anything, and I never should have ruined your life by giving Mom one more reason to leave Nashville."

I looked down at his outstretched hand, considered clasping it and offering forgiveness. Instead, I stepped away from Gracie and pulled my twin into my arms. The comfort that flowed through me was like draping a blanket around my shoulders and wrapping us together. Ours was a bond stronger than any others in our lives. "I forgive you, Kade. And I love you, more than you can possibly imagine."

"I love you too, my brother," Kade said, pulling me just a little tighter. "And I've missed you."

"Since we're all confessing our love for each other—" Laura Miller stepped up to our group, her satin prom dress crinkled from her hands gripping the skirt. "The reason I've been so angry the past two years since Tay moved in and took you away from me was because… I'm in love with *you*."

Laura wasn't talking to me. Her gaze was locked with Gracie's.

Chapter Twenty—Gracie
And Nothing but the Truth

"W-what?" Gracie stepped closer to her former best friend.

"Gracie, I've known I liked girls since middle school, but I never told you because I didn't want to ruin our friendship or the way you thought of me. I always kind of hoped you would someday love me too. So when I saw you with Tay, it kind of… broke my heart. Especially because I could see a connection between the two of you that you never had with Jimmy."

I was stunned. I had suspected she liked girls, but I was surprised to find out that she had loved me as more than a friend. I grabbed her hand tightly in mine. "Laura, I would never think of you any differently regardless of who you love. That's your choice, and it doesn't matter what anyone else thinks about it."

Laura smiled softly and tears fell from each of her sad eyes. "Thank you," she said under her breath.

"I'm sorry that I didn't reach out when our friendship broke to see what was wrong," I said. "You're right, I was caught up in everything about Tay, and that wasn't fair to you after you had been my friend for so many years. I don't know how our friendship would have changed if you'd told me how you really felt about me."

"Yeah, I wasn't sure either, which is why I was scared to tell you," Laura said. "I didn't want to lose you as a friend."

"Well, I'm willing to give our friendship another try if you are," I said. "As long as you promise to go back to being the nice Laura I once knew. No more lies in the school paper. Do real journalism, not magazine gossip-column garbage."

Laura laughed softly and shook her head. "No more lies." She glanced around the group of our friends. "From any of us."

I pulled Laura into a long embrace, glad to have my friend back. But there was one more thing I needed to make clear. I pulled back so we were at arm's length. "I love you too… like a sister. Can you be okay with that?"

"Yeah, I can be okay with that." She nodded, and we pulled each other into another hug.

"Who knows, maybe I can match you up with the right hottie," I said with a wink.

"No more matchmaking!" Taylor exclaimed, and we all laughed.

Chapter Twenty-one—Taylor
Allow Me to Introduce Myself

"Hey, Gracie and Laura." I hated to break up the moment, but I needed to do one more thing to make all this right. I turned to Maddie to include her as well. "I want to introduce myself, since, you know, I'm your next-door neighbor. My name's Taylor Burton, but everyone calls me Tay."

I pulled Kade closer to me and continued my reintroduction.

"This is my twin brother Kade, who I haven't seen in two years because he was healing from some past mistakes. Our dad is Kai Burton, the guitarist for the rock band Buxton Peak. We moved here to get a fresh start, and I would love it if you could be a part of it."

Gracie smiled and stepped forward, putting her hand in mine to return the handshake. "It's nice to meet you, Tay. I'm Gracie Hansen, and these are two of my best friends, Laura and Maddie. I'm glad you moved in next door, and happy to be a part of your fresh start."

I reached out to Maddie. "I heard you have a beautiful singing voice. You and my brother Kade would probably get along great. He's a pretty talented musician."

Maddie shook my hand with a giggle and tucked a lock of hair behind her ear, locking eyes with Kade. "I'm excited to get to know you better, Kade."

"I'm excited to get to know you as well, Maddie," Kade said, taking the hand she'd just released from mine. "You know, a slow song just started in the ballroom. Would you dance with me?"

"I would love to dance with you." Maddie said flirtatiously, and they walked away together, swallowed into the sea of high school kids on the dance floor.

I stepped over to Laura and reached out to her as well. "I heard you're kind of like a sister to Gracie. And any sister of Gracie's is a sister of mine."

"I'm sorry I've been a jerk the past few years," Laura said. "And I'm sorry I printed mean things in the newspaper."

"All is forgiven." We shook, and then I turned to Gracie. "You know, I've had my eye on you all night, and I hoped I could ask you to dance."

"I'd love to dance with you, Tay Burton." Gracie smiled slightly and shook her head. "That's going to take some getting used to."

"Guess we're going to have to spend lots of time together so you can get used to it."

"Tay, can I interrupt for a second?" Laura asked. "Could you, maybe, introduce me to your dad's band sometime? I'm kind of a huge fan."

"I'll do even better than that," I said. "Next time they have a concert within a hundred-mile radius, I'll get us all tickets and backstage passes."

"Thank you so much," Laura said with a huge grin. "You two have fun on the dance floor." She started to back away, but Gracie pulled her in for one more hug.

As we headed over to the dance floor, Gracie called over her shoulder. "You're coming to my tennis match tomorrow, right?"

"Wouldn't miss it," Laura called back.

What had started as the worst night of my life ended with Gracie in my arms on the dance floor, her hands around my shoulders, her wrist corsage resting near my boutonniere. "We match," I said.

"We're a perfect match," Gracie said. Then she lifted onto her toes, and her lips met mine in a perfect kiss.

Epilogue—Kade
Planning for the Future

Maddie and I technically slept together on prom night. Before I brag too much, I should clarify that we were still fully dressed and lying on a grassy knoll near the point of Liberty Park, watching the moon set over the Cumberland River.

My tux was covered in grass, Maddie's prom dress was crinkled, and there were ants in her wrist corsage.

Thankfully, our parents thought we were at the after-prom lock-in so none of them knew.

Not surprising, Gracie called us out when we arrived. "You two look like you didn't sleep at all." There was a teasing glint in her eyes. No doubt Taylor had already ratted us out. Not that I cared.

Prom was lame, Maddie had her own car, so we ducked out halfway through the evening and drove down to the park. We sat and talked, digging our feet into the thick grass, lying on the bank of the river, gazing at the moon and the stars, listening to the water flow past. Yeah, it wasn't surprising Maddie and I fell asleep. I was really starting to like her.

I reached over and wrapped my arm around her waist, pulling her close to me. "Who can sleep when you have this beauty lying next to you?"

Maddie giggled and winked at me before turning to Gracie "We can sleep when we're dead. We weren't going to miss your tennis match against our rivals."

Gracie flashed a huge smile, glancing around our group. Taylor, me and Maddie, and Laura, her former best friend. As of last night, her former friend turned enemy turned friend again. I couldn't keep track. Gracie was probably still on a high from everyone making up.

"How did I get so lucky to have such amazing friends?" Gracie asked.

Taylor wrapped his arm around Gracie's shoulder. "Just don't forget, you and I have officially moved *out* of the friend zone."

"Gag me," I said, rolling my eyes. I was stoked to have my brother back to treating me like his twin, but I don't do mushy. Taylor had always been the more romantic one of us. I had to admit he and Gracie were kind of cute as lovesick puppies. Never for me. That wasn't my style.

"I'm excited for your tournament, Gracie," Laura said with an encouraging smile.

"I wish you were out there playing with me." Gracie pouted.

"Nah, I'm heading up to Central Michigan University in the fall to focus on photojournalism. They have one of the best programs in the world. Tennis was a hobby for me. That's your thing."

"Hey, our Aunt Megan graduated from that college." College. I didn't even really think about how college was supposed to start in just a few months. I never thought about going to college. I didn't see a point when I wanted to pursue music anyway. I wondered if Maddie knew where she was going.

"Tay and I are going to Stanford," Gracie said. "I'm signing my National Letter of Intent on Monday to play tennis there. I'm planning to major in engineering."

"And I'm going to major in environmental science." Taylor puffed up his chest as if that was something to brag about. What a dork I had for a twin brother. He could be an environmental scientist. I was going to be a rock star like our dad.

"Well, it sounds like you three have it all figured out," Maddie said, slumping her shoulders. I wondered what *she* had figured out.

Gracie turned to her coach who was waving her over. "Oh, I've got to go. Wish me luck."

"Good luck," we said in unison, then walked over to the bleachers and sat together to watch Gracie play. Within a few minutes of the tournament starting, Gracie was in control. She ran all over the court, smacking the ball with force.

"I hope I never get on Gracie's bad side," I said to Maddie, who sat by my side. "Because I wouldn't want to be the ball to her racket."

"Right? She's so talented." Maddie didn't take her eyes off her best friend.

I wanted to ask Maddie about her plans for the future because I kind of liked the idea of having her around. Knowing I was planning to head back to Nashville eventually made me nervous. I nudged her shoulder. "So do you know where you're going this fall?"

Maddie wrinkled her nose and shook her head. She

turned to me and said, "I want to pursue a music career, but I don't even know how to get started."

"Well why don't you come to Nashville with me? You could meet my dad's band, and maybe they can connect us with the right people so we can work on music together."

Maddie bit her lower lip and creased her brow, cringing with apprehension. "I don't want you to think the only reason I'm hanging around you is because your dad's a rock star."

I grabbed her hand and waited until she met my gaze. "Maddie, I've been around girls like that. Believe me, you are nothing like them."

Maddie sighed and put her head on my shoulder. I wrapped my arm around her waist and held her tight.

"Where would we even stay?" Maddie asked.

"You could stay at my dad's place with me. It's plenty big enough. There's an amazing pool, multiple wings and stories, and a recording studio where we can work on music together."

"I don't know, Kade," Maddie said. "We barely just met."

"Maddie, I've done way crazier things with people I've known for a shorter amount of time than you."

"That's reassuring," Maddie said sarcastically, with a knowing smile.

"Okay, that's not what I meant," I said quickly. "It isn't like I'm asking you to move in *with me* or anything. The house is enormous. There is even a guest house you could stay in if that would make you feel better."

Maddie nodded as if thinking through all the possibilities. I wasn't just asking her to move an hour away, I was asking her to move into my rock star father's millionaire lifestyle. That's a lot for most people to take in.

"You don't think your parents would mind?" Maddie asked hesitantly.

"Nah. My mom already knows you through Tay and Gracie. And my dad's cool as long as I stay sober."

Maddie closed her eyes and let out a deep breath, then sat up and looked at me. "Yes, I'll go. Let's do this."

"Awesome!" I called out a little too loudly in celebration just as Gracie missed a ball and lost a point. I couldn't contain my smile even as Taylor turned around and punched me in the leg.

"Quiet, moron. This is a tennis match," Taylor growled under his breath.

"Sorry," Maddie and I said together sheepishly.

We turned to look into each other's eyes, and I realized I was starting to fall hard for this girl. Every minute drew me closer to her, and I didn't want to lose her. Being together in Nashville, doing what we both love, was a sure way to make her mine. I raised my eyebrows seductively. "This is going to be awesome. I promise."

Love Letter from Author Julie L. Spencer

Oh, my friends, I love these characters. They are so special to me. I hope you love them too.

A few months ago, when I started writing a book with the main character as a high school tennis player, I asked my friend Audi dozens of questions because she played tennis in high school. She helped me so much that I joked I should put her name on the cover of the book.

Then I thought, Hey! Audi could help write the book! If she's going to have her name on the cover, she might as well get the experience of writing the book. Although I kept final artistic liberty, I gave Audi free reign for the main female character's perspective while I wrote the main male character's perspective.

She truly co-wrote this book with me because she wrote every other chapter! And she helped with all of my chapters just like I helped with all of her chapters!

Although *Matching You with Love* is part of my All's Fair in Love and Sports series, this is a springboard into Audi's first solo series featuring two of the side characters in *Matching You with Love*, Kade and Maddie, and features characters from my Rock Star Redemption Series!

Did you love *Matching You with Love*? The greatest gift you could ever give us is to leave a review on

Amazon and/or Goodreads. Even if you didn't purchase this book for yourself, you can still leave a review. Even just a couple of sentences telling the world what you liked or didn't like can help others decide if they want to read the book. While you're considering whether to leave a review, please enjoy a few chapters of *Almost a Rock Star: Rock Star Redemption Series Book One*.

God bless you, my friends. Stay safe! *-Julie L. Spencer*

Love Letter from
Author Audi Lynn Anderson

Writing this story with Julie has been a whirlwind experience. I have been helping her with her business as an author for over a year now, and to say I have learned a lot is a severe understatement. She gave me such free reign on creating various characters in this story, and also allowed me to help her with hers too. I love the team that we make.

What I am incredibly excited about though is the journey that Kade and Maddie are going to go on together. Their love is gritty, raw, and real. I am a sucker for sappy stories as many people are, but I love the really challenging love stories the most. Love is meant to help us grow into better people, and Kade and Maddie's relationship is sure to do just that.

I hope you enjoy the next story! *-Audi Lynn Anderson*

Almost a Rock Star: Rock Star Redemption Series Book One

Chapter 1 – Child Prodigy Plus Three

– Ian

Ian poked his head through the partially opened door, hoping to eavesdrop.

"Claire, I cannot continue as your son's instructor." Mr. Ashton's voice was firm as he sat across from Ian's mum.

"But… he needs to learn to play the piano." She leaned forward, desperation pulling her shoulders together. "He seems to have a natural talent."

"That's why he needs to move. He's already exceeded my ability."

"Move? Move where?"

"I would suggest Manchester." Mr. Ashton placed two brochures on the table. "Chorlton High School has an exceptional music program where Ian will have the finest instructors. They even have a recording studio on campus."

"High school? He's only eight years old!"

"Yes, I recommend Claremont Primary School in the interim." He pointed to the second brochure. "They also have an excellent music program… although I'd contact the high school as soon as possible and find a private tutor."

"Are you suggesting I drive an hour to take my son to school each day?" Her voice rose an octave by the end of her question.

"Or you could rent a flat and stay during the week."

"That is the most ridiculous thing I've ever heard!" Ian's mum stood suddenly, pushed her chair away— along with her usual proper demeanor—and balled her fists.

"Ian?" Mr. Ashton peeked around Ian's mother. "Could you please come in and sit at the piano?"

"Yes, sir." Ian pushed into the room and obediently settled on the piano bench. *Leave Buxton? Music program? Recording studio?* His heart raced with excitement.

"Now, Claire, what is your favorite hymn?" Mr. Ashton asked.

"*God Save the Queen*," she said.

"Ian, would you please play *God Save the Queen* for your mother?"

Without opening a hymnbook, Ian played the hymn from start to finish, without a single missed note. When he was done, he brushed his shaggy, brown hair off his forehead and smiled at his mum. She dropped into her chair and gaped at him.

"Now, what is your least-favorite genre of music? One you would never play in your home?" Mr. Ashton pulled open the glass door on a shelving unit, revealing rows and rows of colorful CD cases. Ian raised his chin, trying to peek around his teacher at the cornucopia of music.

"Probably jazz," Mum said. "It grates on my nerves."

Mr. Ashton pulled down a case, carefully removed the CD, and loaded it into the player. After pushing a few buttons, he found a song and let the music play for a moment. "Ian, have you ever heard this song?"

"No, sir."

"I want you to listen to it all the way through, as many times as you need, and then play it on the piano."

Ian turned back to the keys and concentrated on the notes while listening to the strange music. He understood why his mum didn't like it. But he saw the notes dance before his eyes, feeling the rhythms and hearing the intricate delicacies of the individual sounds. He listened only once and then placed his fingers on the keys and plunked a little, trying to mimic the song. He stopped. "Could I hear it one more time?"

"Of course." Mr. Ashton started the song over, and Ian listened all the way through again. This time when his fingers danced across the keys, the song was almost flawless.

"An hour isn't such a long drive," his mum whispered.

* * * * * * *

Journal Entry 1: Twelve Years Old

Tomorrow I start Year Seven of secondary school, and I'm really nervous. My mum suggested I start a journal to help me adjust. I've never written in a journal before and I'm not sure I'm comfortable with it. But I'm not sure I'm comfortable going to high school either. I think I'll be okay because I've been going to Chorlton High School for years for private music instructions. My mum hired the band teacher, Mr. Hayworth to be my tutor years ago when I transferred from Buxton to Claremont Primary School. I'll also have my best mate with me, Kai. I haven't seen him all summer. He probably won't even remember me. I hope I don't get into any trouble. I heard the head teacher is really strict. This whole journaling thing isn't helping. It's just making me more nervous. I think I'll go play piano for a little while. That should help me relax so I can go to sleep. Big day tomorrow. Wish me luck! - Signed, Ian Taylor

* * * * * * *

"Stop, stop, stop!" Ian called out above the noise of the high school band. "The bass guitar is out of tune!"

119

Mr. Hayworth lowered his baton, and every head in the crowded band room followed his gaze. "Ian, you can't just interrupt class like this."

Even though he was only twelve, Ian knew every inch of the music rooms, and each instrument within. He'd been coming to Chorlton High School for tutoring since they'd moved to Manchester.

Ian ignored his teacher and mentor. Mr. Hayworth was used to Ian's antics, but many of the kids in year seven were transfer students from schools in Manchester and the surrounding region. The first day of high school was never a good time to cause problems in class. Some mouths gaped, some kids looked annoyed, some amused. All had raised eyebrows.

Ian carefully set down the trumpet he was holding, pushed back his chair, and weaved his way across the room. A kid named Andy stood with a bass guitar in his hands and the strap strapped around his shoulder.

Kai Burton, Ian's best friend from Claremont Primary School, sat next to Andy and held an electric guitar on his lap. Kai's brown eyes sparkled with mischief as he stuck his foot out to trip Ian, and Ian glared at Kai before turning to Andy. Although the guys were playful and impish outside the band room, music was the one thing Ian took seriously.

"May I?" Ian didn't wait for Andy to reply. He just lifted the guitar strap off Andy's neck and slid the bass guitar from his classmate's hands into his own. Expertly sliding the strap into place as if he played every day, Ian sat on a nearby chair and began turning the knobs on the head of the instrument. He strummed a few chords, tightened a few knobs again, played a few more notes, and smiled as he stood to hand the guitar back to Andy. "There you go."

"You're really weird." Andy's smirk told Ian he was grateful rather than annoyed.

As Ian passed Kai, his friend rolled his eyes. "Show-off."

"You're just lucky I tuned yours before class," Ian mumbled on his way to the brass section.

* * * * * * *

Journal Entry 2: Twelve Years Old

School was better than I thought it was going to be. Kai remembered me and was glad to see me. We made friends with a kid named Andy who plays the bass guitar. He's not very good, but he has potential. Maybe I'll tutor him. I'm jealous that Kai gets to sit by him because Kai plays electric guitar. Maybe I'll switch instruments. Mr. Hayworth says I can pick whichever instrument I want. I think I wanna try them all. -Signed, Ian Taylor

* * * * * * *

Journal Entry 3: Twelve Years Old

Some of the kids think I'm weird. I'm a skinny, geeky, music freak who can play any instrument but

121

can't play football. Whatever. At least Kai likes me. He doesn't look at me like I'm weird, like everyone else does. I miss my dad. I live for weekends. -Ian Taylor

* * * * * * * *

Journal Entry 4: Twelve Years Old

School's better, I guess. All I really want to do is stay in the band room. Andy has been nicer to me and of course Kai is my best mate. Mostly everyone else ignores me. I don't care. I just wanna jam. -Ian Taylor

* * * * * * * *

Journal Entry 5: Thirteen Years Old

It's been a long time since I wrote in my journal but school just got out and I'm bummed that I'm going to be away from Kai and Andy for the whole summer. I'm excited to see my dad, though. I'll spend the whole summer home in Buxton. We'll keep our flat in Manchester for when school starts again. Year eight. Wow! -Ian Taylor

* * * * * * * *

Journal Entry 6: Thirteen Years Old

Year eight starts tomorrow. I'm back in Manchester.

122

I didn't write in my journal at all this summer because I forgot my journal at our flat. Oops. All I did was climb the peaks and play piano. I think I sort of learned to write music. I don't write it down or anything so it doesn't really count. The sounds are just in my head. My mum and dad didn't know that's what I was doing. They wouldn't understand. Maybe I'll talk to Kai about it. He'll understand. If he still wants to be my pal. I haven't seen him in months. -Ian

* * * * * * *

Journal Entry 7: Thirteen Years Old

Kai and Andy and I are still best mates! I guess I've grown over the summer because most of the kids in year eight are my size now. Kai is still taller than me, but I don't look so small and geeky anymore. Maybe I'll make some other friends. The kids seem to laugh when I say something funny. Maybe I'll be the funny kid at school. Sincerely, Class Clown

* * * * * * *

"What's your problem, pal?" Kai's voice filled with anger at the kid who had accidentally shoved him against his locker. Ian was shocked by the hatred in Kai's expression. Andy stood at Kai's shoulder and raised his chin.

A year and a half into high school and Kai was a

head taller than most students at Chorlton. At fourteen, he was already filling out like a man. This scrawny boy was no match, but he furrowed his brow and puffed his chest as they locked eyes.

"Excuse me for tripping." The kid narrowed his eyes in hostility. "You shouldn't have left your satchel so far out into the hallway that my feet got caught."

"I can leave my bag anywhere I want." Kai balled his hands into fists as Ian wormed his way in between his best mate and the kid who was stupid enough to cross him.

"Guys break it up." Ian stepped forward, offering himself as the middleman. "You must be new. I'm Ian." Entering a new school halfway through the year was hard enough but getting beat up on the first day wasn't a good way to start things off.

The kid still had his eyes narrowed at Kai. He looked down at Ian's outstretched hand with disdain, but reluctantly shook it. "Gary."

"You've met Kai." Ian gestured with a nod and pulled Andy over into the circle. "… and this is Andy. Come say hello to our new classmate."

"What's up?" Andy raised his chin in reluctant greeting, his sandy brown hair hanging low on his forehead.

"There, now we're all friends," Ian said. "We're going to get on just fine, right?" He raised his eyebrows and looked pointedly at Kai and then Gary.

"Whatever…" Kai turned and sauntered away as if

he owned the hallway. Andy regarded Gary coolly for a few more seconds, looking him up and down, before following Kai.

"It was very nice to meet you, mate." Ian nodded and strode down the hall.

"Ian," Gary called after him. Ian turned back and raised his eyebrows. Gary's expression softened. "Thanks."

"See ya around, Gary."

* * * * * * *

"What instrument would you like to play today?" Mr. Hayworth asked Ian as he walked into class.

"I'm feeling the snare drum," Ian replied, rubbing his chin as if contemplating.

"Oh good, you can help our new kid learn the ropes."

Ian turned toward the back of the room where Gary poked around in the percussion section. "It's Gary."

"Great! You've already met." Mr. Hayworth clapped him on the shoulder, effectively nudging Ian in the direction of the drums.

Ian approached the back of the room, apprising Gary as he did. The kid's sullen expression, and the way his dark brown hair hung low over his eyes, hinted at a troubled past. But Ian wasn't concerned about his mysterious new pal. He wanted to know the important

125

details. "How long you been playing?"

Gary startled, but he regarded Ian. "Since I can remember. You?"

"I don't know." Ian sauntered around a snare drum and picked up a set of sticks. "...A while..." Ian twirled one of the sticks in his right hand, challenging Gary with his eyes and a tiny smirk.

Gary answered Ian's smirk with narrowed eyes and stepped around the opposite snare. He didn't bother with the sticks next to the drum but pulled his own set out of his jacket pocket. They were beautiful, with just the right amount of wear but none of the dents and scratches of the practice sticks. Ian gulped, envious of his new dueler.

"You first," Gary said.

Ian didn't even think as his sticks flew in an intricate rhythm he was sure could never be matched. He never broke eye contact with Gary.

He played for almost a half-minute before stopping, expertly crisscrossing the sticks and holding them steady.

Gary held Ian's eyes and copied the complicated pattern of beats as if they'd been laid out in front of him on a sheet of music. He ended in a similar manner and raised his eyebrows.

"You go first this time," Ian said.

They still hadn't broken eye contact. Ian sensed they'd drawn the attention of other students in the band room. Gary changed up the rhythm and added some

126

complexity, challenging Ian to rise to his level. Ian held his own as he copied Gary's pattern.

When he was nearly finished, Ian nodded just slightly in invitation, and Gary's sticks flew along with Ian's almost as if they were copying each other in perfect synchronicity. It only took a few seconds to realize they were playing the drum solo from *Welcome to the Jungle* by Guns N' Roses. It was just simple enough to be an easy duel for the talented young drummers, but complex enough to be quite impressive to their growing audience. They played through to the end of the solo, and Ian reached over and rolled a simple crescendo on the cymbal.

The entire band room erupted in applause, and amidst the chaos, Ian and Gary reached across and shook one another's hands. Their smirks had become full grins. He wrapped his arm around Gary's shoulder and turned to Kai, who stood beside Andy. An unspoken understanding sparked in their eyes. The four young men regarded one another. Something big shifted in Ian's life. "Mates, I've got a brilliant idea."

* * * * * * *

Journal Entry 8: Fourteen Years Old

A new kid started at our school today. His name is Gary and he plays the drums! Like, really, really well! Kai didn't like him at first until Gary and I played drums together and now Kai likes him, and so does Andy. We're going to start a rock band together! -Ian

Chapter 2 – The High Peak

– Ian

"Let's go to Buxton for the weekend," Ian said to Kai. "I wanna show you guys the view from the High Peak, and I think it would be a good place to get some inspiration. Plus, I haven't seen my dad in a while. I'm glad we have a flat so close to school, but I miss seeing my dad every day." Ian sidled up next to the group of girls by his locker and dialed his combination. Flashing them a quick grin and winking at the cute redhead, he grabbed his geography textbook and slammed the locker closed.

"I've got inspiration right here." Kai brushed off Ian's suggestion and wrapped his arm around a blonde girl named Cheri. "I don't need to climb a mountain."

Ian recognized a lost opportunity and decided to postpone the discussion about his idea. "Ladies, you know you're all beautiful, but if you want to hang out with Kai, you're going to have to come with us to geography class because I *can't* be late. If I get another low mark on an exam, my mum won't let me stay here at Chorlton."

"Oh, Ian," said the little redhead, Janie. "That would be, like, the worst thing that could ever happen." She pouted her lips, batted her eyelashes, and then slipped her hand into his and dragged him in the direction of the geography room.

"Worst ever?" Ian allowed himself to be pulled forward. "We wouldn't want that." He kept his hand in Janie's all the way down the hall until they turned the corner and ran into Headteacher Wallis.

Ian dropped Janie's hand, and the girls stepped away. Public displays of affection were not allowed at school, and the boys were already in enough trouble for skipping Physical Education class the previous week. They'd snuck into one of the practice rooms behind the band room and played guitar for the entire period.

"Ladies, get to class." Mr. Wallis glared at the boys. "Gentlemen, may I have a word with you?"

"Of course, Mr. Wallis." Ian walked down the hall, his arm around his headteacher's shoulders as if he was the one directing the conversation. "Walk with me as I go to geography class."

"You do realize those girls are only fifteen, right?"

"Hmm… that's going to be a problem. I'm only fourteen."

"Dating an older woman, huh?" Kai said from behind them. "You're a stud, Ian."

"Mr. Burton, you're in just as much trouble as Mr. Taylor. I'd watch your mouth, son."

"Ah, Mr. Wallis," Ian said. "We weren't doing anything wrong. The girls just naturally flock to us because we're such nice boys. I'm sure you understand. You were a boy once. Did you have a lot of girlfriends when you were young, Mr. Wallis?"

"Don't change the subject, Ian."

"Well, here we are at geography class. Thank you for escorting us, Mr. Wallis. I'm sure my mum will be grateful I made it here in time." Ian pulled Kai into the classroom, and they sauntered to the back of the room where two empty seats were sandwiched between Gary and Andy.

"That was close," Kai said.

"What'd you do this time?" Andy asked.

"Just a couple of girls." Ian grinned.

"You did *what* to a couple of girls?" Gary's voice was a little too loud and several students' heads turned with wide eyes and gaping jaws.

"Nothing!" Ian shushed them but didn't stop the smile from reaching his eyes. "We did nothing wrong."

Kai put his hands behind his head and leaned back in his chair, propping himself against the back wall of the classroom. He raised his eyebrows at the girl in the desk closest to his and smirked. She blushed and turned around with a soft giggle.

"I kinda like girls," Kai said.

"I know you do, mate." Ian patted his best friend on the knee and faced forward. The teacher strolled to the map and began droning on about Middle Eastern landforms. "I still say we need to visit the High Peak."

*　*　*　*　*　*　*

Journal Entry 9: Fourteen Years Old

I got hit on by a girl today! Her name is Janie and she's really cute with red hair and freckles. She held my hand and almost got me in trouble. Maybe I should erase this from my journal. I'm not old enough to date yet and my mum might get mad at me. It's not like I did anything wrong. Besides my mum's probably never going to read this. If you do read this, Mum, sorry. I like girls, well, I like Janie. I promise I won't do anything except hold her hand. -Ian

*   *   *   *   *   *   *

"The way I see it, people are *not* going to take us seriously unless we can write our own music." Ian tossed a small rock as far as he could and watched it bounce down the hill.

"They're not going to take us seriously until we've grown a foot or two," Andy pointed out.

"You sound like my Sunday school teacher," Ian said. A song from his younger days at church came rushing into his mind, a tune about wanting to serve as a missionary when he was all grown up. *Whatever, that's a long time from now.*

"Seriously though," Kai said. "Just because you two played a tiny little drum duel doesn't mean you can somehow become rock stars. You're just a couple of kids."

"We... are just a *group* of kids." Ian held his hands

out to stop them and get their attention. "We have to include *all* of us in this conversation. Kai, you've played the electric guitar for years. Andy, you can be the bass, and Gary, you obviously would be the drummer."

"What are *you* going to do?" Kai folded his arms across his chest and raised his eyebrows.

"I'll be the singer." Ian nodded once as if it was all decided.

"The only songs you know how to sing are hymns." Kai pushed Ian's shoulder.

"Ugh, why would anyone want to sing hymns? Even at a church." Gary shuttered.

"My grandma made me go to church once," Andy said. "It was really boring."

"I know how to sing more than just hymns," Ian mumbled. He stomped away from them and let them continue their joking. *How can I get them to take this seriously?* Suddenly he jumped onto a large rock and belted out the opening line of *You Give Love a Bad Name* by Bon Jovi.

All three guys looked up at Ian as if he was crazy. No one spoke for a long moment, and then Kai sang up to Ian, continuing the second line of the iconic rock song. They harmonized together "... you give love a bad name."

"You have a great voice," Andy said, his eyes wide. Gary nodded in agreement.

"We need make-out songs." Ian jumped down off

the rock.

"You've never snogged in your life." Kai scoffed.

"That's not the point." Ian stopped him and tried to keep the conversation on track. "We need to make it *seem* as if we know what we're talking about. We need hard rock love songs, breakup songs, that kind of thing."

"Like the boy bands of the nineties?" Gary shook his head. "Yuck, I don't want something my mum would listen to."

"We're not a *boy* band," Ian said. "We're a *rock* band, like Bon Jovi or Aerosmith!"

"Pal, we're not even officially a band," Kai interrupted. "Are we?"

"Why not?" Ian shrugged. "We're talented enough."

"We're barely out of primary school," Kai said. "You haven't even reached puberty yet."

"I have too," Ian said.

"Prove it." Kai folded his arms across his chest.

"How do you *prove* that?"

"Go out with a girl," Kai said, narrowing his eyes and stepping closer to Ian. "I dare you."

"Yeah, and get her past second base," Gary chided.

"You know good Mormon boys don't do that." Ian shook his head. "My dad would kill me."

"Your dad would never have to find out." Andy raised his eyebrows and smirked.

"God would know." Ian nodded definitively.

"I don't believe in God," Kai said. All conversation halted.

Andy tried to get back on track. "All right, all right, so Ian's not going to snog a girl, whatever. What are we going to name our band?"

"What about little Janie?" Gary interrupted. "She probably wants Ian."

"Lots of girls want Ian." Kai pushed Gary's arm. "He's just oblivious."

"I didn't say I'd *never* snog anyone," Ian grumbled. He huffed away, stepping back up on the rock and looking down at the town where he grew up. If he told them what he really thought, they'd laugh.

Ian had been taught as a youth how sacred his body is and how anything more than kissing should wait until he was married. He also knew what girls wanted. He wasn't stupid. He knew what Janie wanted. But more important than that, he knew what God wanted.

I don't care what Kai says. I know there's a God, and he wants me to keep my body and mind pure and focused on what's right and good. He made me, and this earth, and he even made this peak high above Buxton so I could look down and appreciate it… Buxton… Peak. Ian snapped his fingers. *We could name our band after the town where I grew up and the forest that surrounds it. Perfect!*

Ian halted his internal conversation and turned to where the guys were still contemplating whether or not

Ian would *ever* lose his virginity. Ian sighed at their idiocies. "How about Buxton Peak?"

The teasing quieted. They all looked up at him, and the irony of the moment wasn't lost on Ian. He was the musical genius behind this arrangement. He was their leader. He raised his eyebrows and stared directly at his closest friend, Kai.

"I like it." Kai's statement was almost lost to the wind, but Ian heard his words loud and clear. Something in Kai's expression shifted, and they nodded at one another.

"Buxton Peak it is, then." Ian hopped off the rock and pulled everyone together, draping their arms around one another's shoulders. "Let's rock."

"Let's rock," Kai, Andy, and Gary answered.

Buxton Peak was born. They were officially a rock band.

*   *   *   *   *   *   *

Kai says we need to get Twitter accounts, so here goes.

@IanTaylorBP1 tweeted:

My 1st tweet. I have no idea what I'm doing. #My1stTweet #Confused

*   *   *   *   *   *   *

@IanTaylorBP1 tweeted:

#Inspired at the top of the High Peak today with my mates @bp_burton @AndySmithBP1 @bp_owens #BuxtonPeak

* * * * * * *

"Do you want my honest opinion?" George Taylor glanced sidelong at Ian as he drove home from church. Ian sat behind his mum, so it didn't take much effort to have a conversation with his dad.

"Yeah, Dad, I wouldn't have asked if I didn't want to know what you thought." Ian leaned forward and rested his chin on the back of the upholstered seat in his parents' modest sedan. As a geologist and curator at the local museum, George had made a decent living for their family. They didn't have fancy cars or an expensive home, but Ian had never gone hungry.

"They don't share our values, and I'm afraid you're going to make poor choices if you spend a great deal of time with them." This weekend had been the first time George had met Ian's mates. His mum had seen them in passing at school, and even hosted a small dinner for them at their rented flat in the city. But having all the guys sleep over for the weekend was different.

"That's kind of harsh. They're my best pals." Ian folded his arms across his chest and grumbled. "I'm not going to make poor choices."

"What about them? Are they going to make bad choices? Boys who have rock bands get involved in all kinds of negative behavior. Are *they* prepared to deal with temptations like drugs and girls?"

"I dunno," Ian said.

"You have the teachings of the Church as your foundational bedrock," George said. "Do they?"

"Please don't start talking rocks and geology to me, Dad." Ian wrinkled his nose. "We're not at your museum."

"We just want you to be careful." Ian's mum turned completely around in her seat and looked pointedly in Ian's direction. "You know I've always supported your music, but a rock band is walking a fine line. Remember the teachings of your youth, Ian."

"I will, Mum." Ian frowned and scanned the rolling hills between the road and the horizon.

Later that day, they'd be heading back down the mountain for another week at school. He loved coming to Buxton and spending the weekends with his dad, but Ian was increasingly drawn to Manchester.

No, not Manchester, to Chorlton High School. No, it wasn't even that. The band room, the recording studio, the guitars, the microphones, the sound-proof room. The music. The music was calling to him. Like an addiction. *What have I gotten myself into?*

* * * * * * *

137

@IanTaylorBP1 tweeted:

I think I'm addicted to music. Is that possible?

* * * * * * *

Journal Entry 10: Fifteen Years Old

I'm home in our flat in Manchester. Whoa, did I just write that? Home is in Buxton. School is in Manchester. My band room is in Manchester. My instruments are in Manchester. Oh, and my mates are in Manchester. We had a fun weekend. Kai and Andy and Gary all came with me to visit my home in Buxton. Hey, I got it right that time. We climbed the high peak and talked about music. We named our band Buxton Peak because we were on top of the high peak looking down at Buxton. Is that too cheesy? I've decided to stay here next weekend and ask Mr. Hayworth if we can use the sound room to practice some of the music I've been writing. I hope the guys like my music. If not, it's going to be the shortest period of time a band ever existed. -Ian

Chapter 3 – Fine Dining

– Mr. Hayworth

"Are you seeing what I'm seeing?" Marty Hayworth asked his friend. They peered through the window between the sound room and the recording studio, watching the kids manipulate songs and try out different rhythms. His four students were oblivious to their audience.

Jeremy nodded. "How old did you say they were?"

"Ian just turned fifteen. I'm pretty sure the rest of them are all about the same."

Ian frequently paused to write something on a pad of paper and then pulled the guitar back onto his lap. He was clearly giving instructions to the others. They'd been at it since early Saturday morning, taking advantage of an empty school and a band instructor willing to let them into the building. They barely stopped to use the restroom and had not taken a break for lunch.

"Order some pizza," Jeremy said. "We're going to be here for a while."

Marty began to turn away, but he halted and looked down at his long-time friend. "Glad I called you?"

"Worth the drive from London," Jeremy said, smiling up at Marty and raising his eyebrows. "This could get interesting."

* * * * * * *

– Ian

"Oh wow, what smells so good?" Ian looked up to see Mr. Hayworth walk in the door with a strange man who had four pizzas stacked on his arms.

His tailored suit and polished shoes hinted the man was too professional to be a pizza delivery boy, but the other guys didn't seem to notice. They set their instruments aside. Each grabbed a box and headed over to the table, offering enthusiastic appreciation. Ian held back. He sensed there was more to this encounter than dinner. He was right.

"Ian Taylor, I presume?" The man raised his eyebrows, already knowing the answer to his own question. He held the pizza out, halfway between them, inviting Ian to close the distance. "Are you hungry?"

"You're American…" Ian cautiously stood and reached for the box. Once the heat from the pizza flowed through the cardboard, and the smell wafted up to his senses, Ian couldn't resist. He had a slice of pizza in his hand and half-eaten before he could finish his thought, much less request an introduction.

"Forgive my manners." The man nodded. "I'm Jeremy Walker. I'm a friend of Marty's… sorry… Mr. Hayworth, and yes; I'm American."

Ian swallowed the last bite of his first piece and

narrowed his eyes at Jeremy. "What are you doing here?"

"Not messing around, are you, Mr. Taylor?" Jeremy wandered through the instruments, ran his fingers along the high hat on the drum set, and not-so-inconspicuously glanced at Ian's notes. He didn't peruse them long enough to read anything but looked back over at Ian with a knowing expression. "Mr. Hayworth invited me to hear you play."

"You came all the way from America… just to hear us play?" Ian couldn't hide the suspicion from his voice.

"I live in London now." Jeremy pursed his lips and let his statement hang.

"What do you do in London?" Ian leaned against the table behind him, his box left open with only the one piece missing. The other guys had forgotten their pizza temporarily.

"I'm… a manager." Jeremy glanced over at Mr. Hayworth, who was leaning against the wall, arms crossed and a smirk on his face.

"Like, of a business?" Ian asked.

"More like… of musicians." If a pin had dropped in the far corner of the building, they all would have heard it loud and clear. Jeremy wasn't here to deliver pizza, and he wasn't here to visit an old friend.

Ian's breath deepened, and his gaze returned to his teacher and mentor. "Did you invite him here?"

"I did." Mr. Hayworth's head nodded slowly up and

down. He pushed himself away from the wall and sauntered across the room. He stopped in front of Ian before looking him firmly in the eye. "Why don't we have some dinner, and you can tell Mr. Walker about your music?"

"I *am* rather hungry." Ian raised his eyebrows. He glanced between his teacher and this new person in his life, took another piece from the box on the table, and lowered himself onto the nearby chair.

* * * * * * *

"Not without my mates." Ian shrugged out from underneath Jeremy's arm and pushed him away. The darkened hallway, where they were taking a stroll, hid Ian's frustration. *I'm not signing anything without them.*

"They're not half as talented as you are, Ian. They're holding you back." Jeremy stopped walking.

"I don't care. I'm not a solo act." Ian turned around when he realized he'd taken five steps alone. The windows' light on the doors at the far end of the hallway created a silhouette around Jeremy's frame, shrouding his expression. Ian didn't care what this man thought or what claims he made.

"I'm not saying you would have to be a solo act." Jeremy held out his hands in resignation. "We would hire a band to be your backup."

"Then you can hire my mates." It felt so obvious. "I formed a band called Buxton Peak, and we are made up of Ian Taylor, Kai Burton, Andy Smith, and Gary Owens. Take it or leave it, but we are a package deal." Ian pivoted on his heel and walked back toward the band room.

"You're turning down the deal of a lifetime," Jeremy called after him. Ian didn't even hesitate, but as he opened the door, he glanced back at Jeremy.

"No, you are."

*   *   *   *   *   *   *

Journal Entry 11: Fifteen Years Old

So, this just happened. We were playing in the practice room and Mr. Hayworth comes in with this guy named Jeremy and a bunch of pizzas and Jeremy wants to sign us to a record deal or something. He's going to meet with our parents. Maybe we won't be the shortest band that ever existed after all. -Ian

*   *   *   *   *   *   *

"We're in a unique predicament," Jeremy began, looking around the table at each of them in turn. "I think you would all agree that taking your children out to bars and clubs would not be a viable option."

Four sets of parents nodded in agreement. The small meeting room off the main dining area of the restaurant was perfect for a group their size. Ian fiddled with his

143

cloth napkin, wondering if he'd be brave enough to use it to wipe his mouth, or if he would just leave it in a floweret resting near the crystal goblet filled with ice water. He realized he was slouching and pulled himself to a straight back, trying to seem businesslike. His heart was beating so fast he thought his mum could probably hear it from her place in the chair to his right. The other guys didn't seem as nervous.

Ian looked over at Kai, whose maturity showed in his polite, confident smile. Ian needed some of that confidence. Gary's sullen exterior and pursed lips couldn't hide the smirk he passed Ian. Andy's playful eyes danced behind his grin, and Ian couldn't help but return the smile. Just a kid along for the ride. He pulled their excitement across the table, and his shoulders relaxed.

"They're going to eventually need to start playing shows; but for now, it's more important to practice and lay down tracks for the songs they're writing." Jeremy reached for his glass, took a sip, and continued. "They should also learn some cover songs. Until they gain a following, that's what the fans want to hear. We introduce the original tunes a little at a time in the beginning." Jeremy opened a leather binder and picked up an expensive-looking pen.

"Should we have an attorney at this meeting?" Ian's dad sat back with his arms crossed and brow furrowed. Ian observed the change in posture and panicked that his dad was going to mess this up before they started.

"That was to be my next item of business," Jeremy said. "You *will* want representation, because I believe in mutually-beneficial contracts."

The parents glanced around the table at one another, and Ian bit his fingernail. *Lawyers? Contracts? I just wanna play music.*

"The boys seem to think they've officially formed a band," Jeremy continued, tapping his pen lightly against the pad of paper on the table. "There are some questions, however. Who has the rights to the name Buxton Peak? Who has the rights to the songs? From what I've seen in the limited amount of time I've been watching these boys, Ian writes all the songs yet uses the collective 'we' to describe their music. I know that's a touchy subject, but those things need to be decided now to avoid legal challenges later."

Ian gulped and glanced back and forth between Kai, Gary, and Andy. Their grins had left their faces, and there was an almost suspicious air in the room. Ian shrank back into his seat. The guys were yet unaware of the handshake agreements already in place.

"Like I said, we're in a unique situation in that we're catching all of this from square one." Jeremy glanced over at Mr. Hayworth and nodded, passing the authoritative baton.

"Jeremy's right." Mr. Hayworth took a deep breath and sat forward, peering over his glasses at the parents, avoiding eye contact with his four students. He reached for a little pitcher of cream and poured a dollop into his coffee. "Most musical groups don't have trained professionals watching their every move like these kids. Most groups play together for months, and usually years, in a garage or basement, jamming, writing, performing, and *then* they get noticed by professionals. It's to their benefit that I've been privy to Ian's talent since he was very young."

Kai's eyebrows creased, and he sat back in his chair. Andy shrugged his shoulders, and Gary frowned.

Helen Owens interrupted. "My son, Gary, has been playing drums and taking lessons since he was a little boy, long before he came to this high school."

"You're right, Mrs. Owens." Mr. Hayworth nodded. "I was very impressed with him from the day he stepped into my band room. But… he's not writing the music."

Helen sat back and folded her arms, pursing her lips and looking over into the far corner. Gary picked at his cuticle and wouldn't meet Ian's gaze.

"Herein lies the challenge," Jeremy cut back into the conversation. "This all needs to be decided *before* we go any further. I have some suggestions on how to draw up contracts for things like this, but I'm not sure I've *ever* been in a situation where I've seen such definitive proof of ownership rights."

Ownership rights? What does he mean? I tell the guys what to play and how to play it, and they play the chords, hold the rhythms, tatt out the beats. Does that mean I own the music? Is that even possible?

"Unfortunately, a fifteen-year-old can't legally enter into a contract. That, coupled with Ian's continued use of the collective when referring to the band, is why I invited all four sets of parents to join me this evening. If we can agree on some terms, start making long-term plans, including escape clauses so everyone feels represented, I think we're on the right track."

"Are you saying what I think you're saying?" John Burton put his arm around Kai's shoulder in support of his son. "That our boys have enough talent that you are willing to represent them before they've ever played a show?"

Ian's head whipped back over toward Jeremy, and their eyes met. Ian knew what Jeremy's true feelings were on the subject of talent. He hoped his piercing gaze spoke to Jeremy's conscious. *Lie if you must. Don't mess this up!*

"Well, that would be drawn into the contract," Jeremy explained. "I want them to have representation *before* they get that far so they can hit the ground running, so to speak. But yes. There is a great deal of talent in this room."

Good save! Shoulders relaxed around the table. The parents glanced at one another, small smiles showing here and there, with some skepticism, some suspicion, but all ears were opened to Jeremy's ideas. Ian gulped. *Is this really happening?*

"Here's where I see this going," Jeremy said. "The guys will continue as they are, writing, practicing, recording, and learning the music business. Then, when they're ready, in maybe a year or two, they begin playing locally at small venues, such as a community theater or small stadium."

"Stadium?" Ian spoke for the first time that evening. "Like, with people paying money to get in?" Most of the adults in the room chuckled.

"Duh," Kai said. "That's the idea." The corner of Ian's mouth lifted in response to his best friend's gleaming eyes. They raised their eyebrows at each other.

"Do you think people will actually come to hear us play?" Andy asked.

"I've been in this business a long time," Jeremy said. "I wouldn't be sitting at this table right now if I didn't think you had what it takes."

"And I wouldn't have called Mr. Walker had I not thought the same." Mr. Hayworth looked around the table at each of the boys in turn. "But it's going to take hard work and determination. Do you think you can handle that?" Ian and the other guys echoed one another's nods of affirmation.

At that point the two waitresses who had been assigned to their table came around with salad and breadsticks, and conversation evolved to other topics. Ian sat back and watched the adults discuss the arrangement. His mind was elsewhere, on a stage, in front of thousands, playing music he'd created.

Ian kept glancing at the other guys with knowing smirks and nodding heads. Let the adults work out the logistics. *Let's rock!*

Want to read more? Buy *Almost a Rock Star: Rock Star Redemption Series Book One* on Amazon.

Acknowledgments

Lisa Rector, I could never thank you enough for your editing skills. You truly save me time and again from publishing stories with huge, gaping holes, and commas in all the wrong places.

Thanks, Brenda Walter for another fabulous cover design. You outdo yourself over and over.

Audrianna Anderson, thank you for being my right-hand woman, administrative assistant, personal assistant, virtual assistant, social media coordinator, sounding board, cheerleader, sometimes-counselor, and true friend.

Thank you, Lara Wynter, for reading my books from the other side of the world and telling me how this story would be different if told from Australia. Also, for helping me fix some things to be more understandable for my international readers. Let's rock!

To my Chapter-A-Day super fans, particularly Joel Rees, Laura Palmer, Paula Hurdle, Bonnie Congrove-Fritz, Teya Peck, Julie Berryman, Lori Smith, Sally Pomerantz, and Crissy Holland. You give me a reason to write every day and fix my mistakes on the fly.

Most especially, thank you to God and to my husband, children, and family. You are my inspiration.

-Julie L. Spencer

Julie L. Spencer and Audi Lynn Anderson

About the Author

Julie L. Spencer writes gritty clean fiction with snarky, flawed characters, and romantic twists and turns. She has over 30 publications, and the books just keep writing themselves. A scientist by day and moonlighting as an author, Julie is an indoor girl with very little desire to step away from her computer and loves her characters almost as much as she loves her kitten.

Sign up for Julie's email newsletter at
www.subscribepage.com/author-julie-spencer

Julie loves to hear from her readers and can be reached at
julie@spencerpublishingLLC.com

Check out Julie's website at:
www.authorjuliespencer.com

Julie L. Spencer and Audi Lynn Anderson

About the Author

Audi Lynn Anderson is an up-and-coming romance author with over 30 books in the works planned over four series. A natural storyteller, Audi has travelled the United States and Europe, and is married to a Second Lieutenant in the US Army who is just starting into medical school. She's also a busy mom raising an energetic and brilliant three-year-old.

Join Audi's weekly email book club at
www.subscribepage.com/x3g9r8

Audi loves to hear from her readers and can be reached at
author@audilynnanderson.com

Check out Audi's website at:
www.audilynnanderson.com

Julie L. Spencer and Audi Lynn Anderson

Matching You with Love

Other books by Julie L. Spencer:

All's Fair in Love and Sports Series

Running to You

Meet Me at Half Court

Pass Me the Ball

Basketballs and Mistletoe

Strike Three, You're Mine

Cheer for Me

Catching Waves with You

Matching You with Love

(with co-author Audi Lynn Anderson)

Royal Family Saga Series

Billionaire Crown Prince

Billionaire Hero

Billionaire Professors (The Geek Twins)

Billionaire's Brother

Billionaire's Sons

Julie L. Spencer and Audi Lynn Anderson

Love Letters Series

Who Wants to Marry a Mormon Girl?
Who Wants to Marry a Billionaire Gamer?

Rock Star Redemption Series

Almost a Rock Star
Billionaire Rock Star
International Rock Star
Fallen Rock Star
Forever a Rock Star
Opening Act: Infusion Deep Meets Buxton Peak
(with co-author, Lara Wynter, Free on Amazon)

Christian Women's Fiction

The Cove
The Man in the Yellow Jaguar
The Farmer's Daughter

Young Adult Social Issues
Combustion

Listen to audiobooks by Julie L. Spencer:

All's Fair in Love and Sports Series

Running to You on Audible
Meet Me at Half Court on Audible
Pass Me the Ball on Audible
Basketballs and Mistletoe on Audible

Love Letters Series

Who Wants to Marry a Mormon Girl? on Audible
Who Wants to Marry a Billionaire Gamer? on Audible

Rock Star Redemption Series

Almost a Rock Star on Audible
Billionaire Rock Star on Audible
International Rock Star on Audible
Fallen Rock Star on Audible
Forever a Rock Star on Audible

Julie L. Spencer and Audi Lynn Anderson

Christian Women's Fiction

The Cove on Audible
The Man in the Yellow Jaguar on Audible

Made in the USA
Columbia, SC
31 May 2021